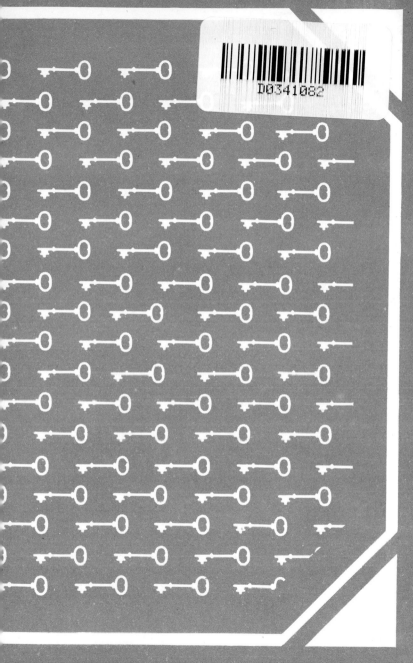

The Sea Has Her Secrets

Girls' MYSTERY Stories

The Sea has her Secrets

by Ian Maclaren

TABLE OF CONTENTS

Chapter 1

Joanna's Ghosts

"I wish I'd gone to the Algarve with my parents. They're staying in a five star hotel this year, you know." Alyson Jones sniffed in what she imagined was a superior manner. "I mean – fancy going to Yorkshire of all places!"

Sally Barnes curled her top lip in a fair imitation of the other girl and in a terribly posh, nasal voice said, "I couldn't agree with you more, Alyson. You should be staying in a five star hotel." Sally's big blue eyes were wide and innocent as she leant over the table in the railway compartment and patted the red-haired girl's hand. "In fact, I'd like to see you staying in a six star hotel – or a seven star hotel – anywhere in the world except with us in Yorkshire."

Joanna and Katie, the other girls in the compartment, seemed to be having trouble with their throats as they hid behind their handkerchiefs, red faced and coughing. "I mean," Sally raised an eyebrow and eyed the two other girls haughtily. "Imagine having to live for two whole weeks with peasants!"

"Why Sally ..." Alyson started to smile then, as

11

the other girl's words sank in, her face flushed a deep red. "I should have known better!" The posh accent vanished. "I should have known better than to sit with you lot. You've always been jealous of me!" She pursed her tight little lips and turned to stare at the passing scenery.

Giggling, Katie removed her spectacles and polished them with her handkerchief, then dabbed at the tears of mirth in her eyes. "This peasant is going to the buffet car," she announced, still with a trace of laughter in her voice. "Can I bring you lot anything back?" She held out her large square hand. "Cash in advance."

"Yes please," Joanna said eagerly. "I'll have two packets of salt and vinegar crisps, a can of fizzy orange and – and ..." she screwed up her pretty face and her black eyes narrowed in concentration, "and a packet of chocolate buttons."

Sally stared at the dark-haired girl as she fumbled in a pocket for her purse. "I don't know how you do it! You eat enough for three normal people, and you still have a figure like a badly tied piece of string!" Sadly she shook her head, her long blonde hair flopping about from side to side. "One day, it's all going to catch up with you." Her voice became sad with just the hint of a sob in it. "And you're going to explode – pow – just like that! All we'll have to remember you by is a huge pile of empty crisp packets!"

While Joanna was counting her money into Katie's outstretched hand, Sally turned to Alyson, who was still sulking in the corner seat. "What about you, Alyson? Do you want anything from the buffet?"

Alyson hesitated, the thought of food successfully overcoming her resentment. "If they have any fresh peaches ..."

"Come on, Alyson," Kate giggled. "This is the five o'clock to Chertsea, not the Orient Express. If they have any fruit at all it'll be apples or oranges."

"All right, then." Alyson brought out her purse. "I'll have a packet of crisps and a fizzy orange."

"What about you, Sally?"

"I don't think I'll bother," Sally smiled. "It's not that long since lunch, and we'll be having supper at seven." Sally's mother was a widow and, though they didn't go short of anything, they didn't have money to throw about.

"You're not slimming, are you?" Katie stared down enviously at Sally's trim waist. "Why, you're as thin as a skeleton as it is ..."

"Speaking of which," said Joanna, her eyes shining with mischief, "I heard that this old school we're going to stay in in Chertsea is haunted!"

"Naturally," Sally sighed exaggeratedly. Everyone in the school knew about Joanna's fascination for ghosts. "If you're going there, it's got to have a vampire or a werewolf or a witch. Maybe all three."

"Why not three of each?" Katie stood up to go to the buffet car. "That's how she usually has her packets of crisps." She made a face at the other girls. "I'm off before she gets started."

Alyson leaned forward to peer intently at Joanna. "This is another of your horrible jokes, isn't it? There isn't really a ghost at Chertsea school, is there?"

"No." Joanna answered cheerfully and the other girl relaxed. "There's twenty three of them!"

"What?"

Sally kicked Joanna's ankle under the table. "Joanna, behave yourself. You know how nervous Alyson gets. A

13

joke's a joke, but you don't want to spoil her holiday, do you?"

"It's not a joke, Sally, I read up on it last night in my ghost atlas. You know, the one that tells you where all the best hauntings are. Alyson was talking about a five star hotel a while ago, and I reckon this is a real first class, five star haunting."

Sally tried to warn Joanna off with her eyes, but once the dark-haired girl got going on her pet subject, there was no stopping her.

"Back in 1736, a merchant ship – the *Sally Hanson* – foundered on the coast near Chertsea village. It's a treacherous coastline up there. There were twenty three people on board, and they were all drowned. Now comes the interesting bit. The authorities suspected wreckers were at work because the *Sally Hanson* was carrying a valuable cargo of silks and gold bullion – and none of it was ever recovered. They never proved anything but, from that day to this, those twenty three souls lost with the *Sally Hanson* have been seen, time and time again, in and around the village." Her eyes were magnetic and she dropped her voice to a whisper. "And until their deaths are avenged, they will continue to haunt the village of Chertsea."

Even Sally who knew Joanna and her stories of old was held for a moment by the power of the girl's hypnotic, whispering voice.

Alyson was in a trance.

"There were twenty three of them," Joanna added, matter of factly. "Twenty two crew and one passenger– the captain's wife." She did her Stan Laurel impression. "So there!"

Sally laughed, but Alyson stared at Joanna with horrified eyes and a half open mouth. "And – and are they all horrible and dead with seaweed in their hair and their clothes all dripping wet?"

"You're thinking of a film, Alyson." Sally tried to break the spell. "It was on TV a couple of weeks ago. I didn't see the end of it because Mum made me go to bed ..."

"Twenty three poor drowned souls," Alyson's eyes were distant and her voice sounded strange, "and they're coming to ..."

"Alyson! Whatever is the matter with you?" Miss Parson's sharp voice sliced through Alyson's trance like a cold steel knife. "Are you feeling all right?" The long, thin teacher stared down at the girls.

"I – I ..." Alyson shook her red head, a dazed expression on her face. She looked round her, puzzled, then – as her eyes alighted on Joanna – her voice hardened and her eyes narrowed spitefully. "It was her!" she said accusingly, pointing a pudgy, freckled finger at the dark, gypsy-looking girl. "She's been trying to frighten me to death with her stories about drowned sailors haunting this school we're going to stay in."

Miss Parson's face assumed its normal look of resigned patience as she laid a hand on Joanna's thin shoulder. "Really, Miss Carter, I'm surprised at you. You know how sensitive poor Alyson is."

"Sensitive!" Joanna exploded. "Why she's got as much feeling as a rhino with a double skin!"

"And as for you, Sally..." Miss Parson's pale, washed out blue eyes were turned sorrowfully on the tall, blonde girl. "I am surprised that you, of all people, would let Joanna talk to Alyson like that." She pursed her thin lips primly.

15

"I know Joanna needs a keeper, Miss Parson, but it's not me," she protested. "Besides, it was a joke."

"Alyson did not find it amusing, young lady." It was back to the classroom with Miss Parson giving yet another of her familiar lectures. "We have to remember we are ladies, and the world will judge us by what we say and what we do. I know it's a modern craze to make fun of everything, but we must remember that what we consider a joke may give offence to others."

It was usually good for ten minutes relief break from domestic science, but this was supposed to be the beginning of the holiday.

"I'm sorry, Miss Parson." Sally took advantage of the teacher's pause for breath to get in with her own set piece. "I'll make sure it doesn't happen again." She looked down demurely to avoid the mischief in Joanna's sparkling black eyes. One look at them and she'd collapse in giggles.

"Good." Miss Parson made a steeple of her long, bony fingers and looked over the top of it at Joanna. "And you, Miss Carter? Are you going to apologise to Alyson?"

"I'm sorry, Alyson." Heroically Joanna kept her face straight, adding under her breath, "I'm sorry I didn't tell you about cold, wet hands reaching out to touch you in the middle of the night. I'm sorry I didn't tell you about staring eyes and skulls and rotting bones ..." She smiled angelically, but Sally could read her thoughts. "But don't worry, Alyson, I'll get round to telling you!"

"Now girls," Miss Parson was smiling at them thinly. "Don't you think it right that you leave Alyson by herself for a while since she isn't feeling too well?"

Nobody was ever sent out of the domestic science

class. Miss Parson was far too refined and genteel ever to descend to the level of the other teachers and punish her pupils. Instead, she would assume that patient, pained, long-suffering look and suggest that perhaps it would be a good idea if the 'young lady' – usually Katie or Joanna – found a reason to be out of the classroom until the end of the lesson. Joanna and Katie had never got round to learning about boiled eggs – never mind fairy cakes.

"Perhaps you'd like to go and sit in the next compartment?"

There was a nasty hint of triumph hovering round the corners of Alyson's tight little mouth as Sally and Joanna got to their feet and collected their things together watched by the mournful Miss Parson. 'More in sorrow than in anger' might have been coined for her.

"A breath of fresh air would do me the world of good," Joanna declared, with her hand on the handle of the door that connected the two compartments. The words were innocent enough, but Sally knew what she meant.

Sally got out of the compartment and pulled the door behind her, before the giggles caught up with her.

"This is another fine mess you've got me into." She leaned her back against the door laughing.

"I'm sorry, Olly." Joanna ruffled her short black hair with her hand. "But you didn't tell me Alyson was so sensitive." She flopped down in a seat giggling.

"Maybe we should try being nicer to Alyson," Sally said, as she sat down in the corner seat, the laughter gone from her face. "This is the second time this year her parents have gone off on holiday without her."

"If I was her parents, I'd be off to Australia – with a one way ticket!"

"Try not to upset her, Joanna, please."

"I'll try, Sally, but she can be such a – a pain!" She smiled. "Well, now we're on our own, how about a game of Scrabble? You can give me a start of fifty points."

"Why don't we wait for Katie?"

"Why?"

"If we start now, she's going to arrive and insist we start again."

"She should be back with my crisps by now."

"Maybe she heard how you upset Alyson and has given your scoff to her as compensation?"

"Not a chance. Katie hates Alyson more than I do." Joanna glanced at her watch. "Let's see. She should be back by now. At this moment, she's dishing out the goodies. Now she's asking where we are. She's being told. Now twenty seconds to get thrown out. Nineteen, eighteen, seventeen . . ."

She'd got to 'five' when the door to the next compartment opened and Katie, clutching an assortment of food and drinks to her chest, backed through the corridor between the compartments doing what she usually did – talk!

"Sorry, Miss Parson, but all I said was that I didn't get her bacon flavoured crisps because I disapprove of cannibalism."

The door slid shut with a bang.

18

Chapter 2

The Sinister Station

"No. You can't have that," Katie declared triumphantly. "It begins with the letter 'K'."

"Not if it means people who nick things," Joanna hugged herself with glee as she started to tot up her score.

Sally smiled as the other two squabbled over the Scrabble board. Because they knew she often played with her mother, they always insisted that she give them fifty points start each, then, against all the rules, they'd team up against her. Miss Parson's notions of how young ladies should conduct themselves had not percolated through to Joanna and Katie – probably because they'd never spent enough time in her classroom to hear them.

Sally knew how to cope with her friends. All she had to do was bide her time and, sooner or later, the two of them would fall out. Then she could get in with the big words and beat them yet again.

The seven letter word was a long time in coming today, however, and Sally's brow was furrowed in concentration when she felt the train begin to slow down.

"We're early if this is Chertsea." A quick glance at her watch confirmed they were nearly seven minutes before time.

"Oh, what a shame!" Katie was gleeful because they were going to have to scrub the game and she had been losing. She swept all the letters off the board and into the bag.

While the brakes squealed and the carriages jerked and bumped, the three girls gathered their belongings together. Luckily, their suitcases and heavy luggage had been sent on separately, so all they had to worry about were coats and brollies and the things they needed on the journey.

A final jolt and the train was at a standstill in a small, deserted station. Joanna wiped a space clear on the dusty window and peered through.

"There's a sign there but the sun's behind it and I can't see ..."

"Put on your sunglasses, then." Katie was trying to cram the Scrabble board into her small hold-all. "Don't you ever watch the adverts on TV?"

"Let me look –" Sally was thrown back in a seat as the train jolted forward.

"Quick! It's starting to pull out!" Katie threw open the carriage door. "Hurry!"

Sally, clutching her cardigan in one hand and her carrier bag in the other was nearly thrown off her feet when the train jolted forward again.

"It *is* Chertsea!" Joanna shrieked. Grabbing Sally by the shoulders, she bundled her towards the door. "And the train's moving!"

True enough, the coach was travelling forward slowly as Sally and Joanna followed Katie in a heap on to the platform. Sally only had time to reach out and slam the carriage door as the train, moving more smoothly now, pulled away from the station.

"Wow!" Joanna mopped imaginary sweat from her brow with the back of her hand. "That was close."

Sally looked round the deserted platform, then her blue eyes came back to rest on Joanna.

"Don't you think we've lost something?" she asked, with deceptive calm. "Isn't there something we should have with us that's still on the train?"

Joanna checked that she had her jumper and her carrier bag then turned to Katie. "You haven't forgotten the Scrabble, have you?"

"No." Katie checked her hold-all once more to be on the safe side. "Why, what is it you think you've lost, Sal?"

"Not a lot," Sally smiled. "Just thirty seven school chums and six schoolteachers."

"You don't think . . . ?" Behind her spectacles, Katie's green eyes were huge and round. "You don't think . . ."

"I think we ought to check that sign again." Without waiting for an answer, Sally strode back down the platform to look up at the sign. Then she turned to Joanna accusingly.

"It's not my fault . . ." Joanna backed away from the other two. "I mean, the top of the board's dirty and I was looking into the sun at the time . . ."

"This is Little Chertsea, dum dum, not Chertsea! It's the wrong station!"

"She's interested in cemeteries and things, isn't she?" Katie turned to Sally and indicated Joanna with her thumb.

"Yes." Sally nodded her head.

"Then don't you think we should give her some first hand experience and send her to stay in one?"

21

"After we've strangled her, of course."

"Of course . . ."

"Come on, Sal, and you, Katie. Don't tell me you've never made a mistake."

"Oh, we made a mistake all right. A big mistake . . ." Sally started.

"Having anything to do with you!" Katie finished for her.

"I think we should find out if there's another train through to Chertsea." Sally turned away from Joanna and started to trudge down the deserted platform towards the ticket office.

"Oh, can't we sort out Joanna first?" Katie wailed. "I haven't had any really good fun for ages." But she, too, turned and followed the tall, slim figure of Sally towards the ticket office.

A very subdued Joanna followed them both.

Not only was the station deserted, but it had a neglected air, as though it hadn't been used for years. The windows in the waiting room were boarded up and the chocolate machines were empty – as Joanna was the first to discover.

There was no sign of life at the ticket counter, the shutter over the paying-in window being pulled shut and looking as though it had been that way for a very long time.

The bell didn't work either, so, in the end, Sally was reduced to pounding on the shutter with her fist bringing down a rain of dust on the girls.

"Shh!" Sally held up her finger to her lips as the other two girls squealed their protests. "I'm sure I heard something moving behind there."

"Probably one of Joanna's ghosts," Katie tittered nervously.

22

"There's got to be someone here." Sally gave a final bang on the shutter with her fist. "Come on, let's look round the back."

"You two go round the back." Katie was looking nervously at the lengthening shadows as the sun sank low in the west. "I'll stay here and look after the bags."

"All right." Joanna winked at Sally. "And if you see any ghosties or long legged beasties while you're here – on your own – give us a shout."

"Or a scream," added Sally.

"Wait! I'll come with you."

They walked past unpainted walls with faded, out of date posters hanging from them in tatters, weeds sprouting through the concrete of the platform and a family of ducks basking in the rays of the late afternoon sun on the opposite platform.

At the back of the building, they found a door with blistered peeling paintwork and a barely readable sign which read, 'Keep Out. Staff Only'.

"Keep out. Staff only," Joanna read aloud.

"Wow!" Katie said in mock surprise. "She got it right this time."

"We'll teach her joined up writing next," Sally laughed as she put her hand on the doorhandle and pushed.

The door swung slowly, creakily open on protesting door hinges to reveal a dim, dusty room full of old, broken furniture. Cautiously, Sally poked her head through the doorway, being crowded by Katie and Joanna into the interior. Her feet on the floor sent up clouds of specks of dust which floated lazily in the air, catching the stray beams from the sinking sun which penetrated through the grimy window.

"Hello?" Sally's voice was thin and nervous. "Is there anyone there?"

"What's it to do with you?" A deep voice boomed out from the dark interior. "Can't you read?"

Katie giggled and whispered, "Not all of us."

"Didn't you see the sign on the door? It says keep out. It says that door is for staff only. You staff are you? Eh?" A short, dumpy figure limped awkwardly out of the shadows, head cocked to one side and face turned away from Sally. He was buttoning a shabby old raincoat right up to the neck. "Eh? Speak up!"

"I – er – I ..." Sally cleared her throat. "We didn't know if there was anyone in here," she started nervously.

"We, girl? Who's we?"

Sally looked behind her, astonished to find she was in the room on her own, there being no sign of Joanna or Katie.

"And if there hadn't been anyone here?" the deep voice, so incongruous from such a short, dumpy figure, almost shouted. "Help yourself to a few things, eh? That what it is? Maybe steal a few things, eh?"

"Certainly not!" Indignation overcame Sally's nervousness. "We were looking for the stationmaster or a porter."

"Won't find 'em in here, gal, won't find 'em in here!"

"Where then? There was no reply at the ticket office."

"You get on back round there, quick like. Bang harder 'cos he's a bit mutt and jeff. Know what that means, gal?"

"Deaf?"

"Not as stupid as you try to pretend, eh? You get round there ... quick!" As he finished speaking, the man shuffled forward and, for one heart stopping instant his face was in the full light of the dying day. He had one eye that was white and obviously sightless, while the other was dark and sparkling with malevolence. His white, haggard face was set in a snarl that showed long, yellowing teeth beneath a straggling grey moustache.

Sally backed away rapidly, the only thought in her mind that he might put out one of those long, gnarled hands with the dirty fingernails and touch her.

An involuntary shudder shook her whole body as she stood outside on the platform and the door slammed in her face. Still shaking, she stood rooted to the spot as a key turned in the lock and she heard a muffled snort from the other side of the door.

If she hadn't known better, she would have sworn it was a laugh.

"Sal!" Katie's shout brought Sally out of her trance. "Round here."

Eyes blazing, the tall blonde girl strode round to the front of the building to where Joanna and Katie were standing by the ticket window. "Some friends you two are!" she fumed. "Leaving me on my own!"

"I didn't leave you on your own." Katie was all innocence. "I left you with Joanna. I only came round here to check that the bags were all right."

"How come, then," Joanna jeered as she put her face very close to Katie's, "that I was already here checking them when you got here?"

"All right then!" Katie stood up to her full five feet two. "I was checking that you were checking them properly. We've already had an example of how well you read today!"

Joanna swallowed her retort as with a squeaking, complaining sound, the shutter over the ticket window was raised.

"What do you want?" The creaky, querulous old face

that peered short sightedly through the window at Sally matched the complaining tone exactly. "Speak up. I can't hear you."

"That's because I haven't said anything yet!"

"No need to shout! I'm not deaf."

"When is the next train to Chertsea?" Sally spoke slowly and distinctly.

"How did you get here?" He peered at her through the murky glass, his head on one side so that he looked like a demented budgie. "Have you got tickets?"

"We came by train. Got off at the wrong stop. Should have got off at Chertsea, not Little Chertsea."

"He, he. Not the first and you won't be the last." Then he stopped cackling and his expression became suspicious. "Where's your tickets?"

"They're still on the train with our luggage and the rest of our party. They've gone to Chertsea."

"You a foreigner? Why're you talking like that, all slow and loud?" He screwed up his face and, for one dreadful second, Sally thought he was going to expel his dentures.

"Is there another train to Chertsea? What time?"

"Seven o'clock."

Sally glanced at her watch and heaved a sigh of relief. It was six fifteen.

"Tomorrow morning." From the malicious expression on the man's wrinkled face, Sally knew he had done it deliberately.

"Is there a bus then?"

He shook his head.

"Taxi?"

"Yes, but that's in Chertsea." He was enjoying this.

"Is there a public telephone?"

"Aye."

"Where?"

"Out there." He pointed to the exit. "But you can't go out there till I see your tickets."

Sally closed her eyes and took several deep breaths.

"I say, my man." Katie tapped on the counter imperiously. "If you don't mend your ways and give us some help, I shall report you for insolence. You are being deliberately obstructive."

"I . . ."

Katie took out the Scrabble score card and a pencil. "I see you're not wearing a regulation uniform, so you'll have to tell me your name and number. Oh, and what position do you hold here?"

The man's face went red, then purple. He glared at Katie then opened his mouth to speak and Sally got prepared to close her ears. She was too young to listen to language like that. Then it was as though he had had a sudden thought. He slammed down the shutter and Sally could have sworn she heard murmured voices behind it.

The shutter went back up again and the wrinkled, prune like face appeared again, the corners of his mouth turned up in what appeared to be a very painful smile. It was certainly hurting him.

"I'm sorry, young ladies." The words were gritted out. "I was just having a little joke with you."

Joanna and Sally stared in astonishment at Katie who had a very smug expression on her face. It would be murder to live with her for the next few days.

"That's all right, my man." Katie was doing her Lady Muck impression. "If you'll give us the number of Chertsea station and tell us the best way to get there, we'll say no more about it."

The old man told them the telephone number of the station and even changed a pound coin to give them some coins.

"Now the best way to get to Chertsea is to go into Little Chertsea, that's about a mile up the road there, turn right at the crossroads and it's signposted all the way."

"Excuse me," Joanna looked puzzled. "But according to my atlas, Chertsea's on the coast. Wouldn't we be quicker following the coast road?"

"No, miss, no." The old man shook his head vigorously. "Don't go along that coast road. It'll be dark soon, and it's a dangerous road."

"It won't be dark for ages, yet." Sally looked at her watch, then at the evening sky. "How long will it take to get to Chertsea?"

"No more'n two hours." He lowered his voice conspiratorially, "That's if you go my way." He looked around as though afraid of being overheard. "Go by the coast road and there's no guarantee that you'll ever get there!"

"What are you getting at?" Sally was beginning to get bored with this old man.

"There's things best not spoke of." He laid his finger alongside his nose. "But if you'll take my advice, you'll stay well away from the coast road tonight." He pulled down the shutter.

"Well? What do you make of that?" Sally looked at the other two.

"I don't think he wanted us to go by the coast road," said Katie, "and I don't think I want to go by the coast road."

"Let's phone the station." Sally started towards the gate.

"I wonder why he didn't phone the station for us?" Joanna looked puzzled.

"Maybe his fire's gone out." Sally put on her disgusted look when the other two didn't laugh. "He's so ancient he probably still uses smoke signals."

Carrying all their belongings, the three girls walked out of the railway station.

Chapter 3

Phantoms From The Deep

"Where are you?" Miss Parson sounded even more like Miss Parson on the telephone. "We've been so worried about you."

"I'm sorry, Miss Parson, but we got off the train at Little Chertsea instead of Chertsea. It's only a few miles away."

"But how ..."

"We'll explain all that when we see you, Miss Parson. The main thing is that you should know we're all right."

"I'll have to explain to the Head. She left me here on the station on the off chance that you would either turn up or get a message to us. Now, how are you going to get here?"

"We'll have to walk."

"Walk? I couldn't hear of that! I'll send someone for you."

"Sorry, Miss Parson, we're running out of change ..." Which was true, and would avoid a long distance lecture. "Don't worry. We'll see you in a couple of hours." The pips went and Miss Parson's protests were cut short.

"I don't see why I always get elected to do all the dirty work." Sally came out of the kiosk annoyed. "One of you two could have made that call."

"Come off it, Sal, you know old Parson thinks we're not playing with a full deck. She thinks you look after us." Joanna grinned craftily. "You know you're her favourite out of us three."

"Sally, how can you let Miss Wallace and Miss Carter behave like that?" Katie steepled her fingers and peered at Sally over the top of them, her spectacles on the end of her nose. "I expected better of you, of all people."

"All right." Sally looked along the road towards Little Chertsea. "Do we take that man's advice and go that way?"

"No," Joanna said promptly.

"Yes," Katie said firmly.

"Looks like it's up to you to decide, Sal." Joanna put her hand on Katie's shoulder. "But if you're going to make me walk an extra couple of miles because this little mouse here is nervous ..."

"I'm not making any decisions." Sally pursed her lips. "You decide."

"All right." Katie reluctantly took a ten pence piece from her pocket. "I'll toss, you call, Joanna."

"No. I'll toss and you call."

At that moment, Sally came very close to walking off and leaving them both to argue, but she knew if she did that, they would follow her and then, once again, she would have chosen for them.

Instead, she folded her arms and watched.

They decided to toss up for who should toss up, but they couldn't agree as to who should toss up the coin to decide who should toss up the coin.

"I'm not interfering," Sally burst out at last, "but since I want to get to Chertsea before the end of the holiday, do you mind if I make a suggestion?"

"As to which way we should go?" Katie asked eagerly.

"No!" Sally was very definite about that. "You make the decision. Then, if anything goes wrong, just for once you won't be able to blame me. There's a blackbird sitting on that tree. Wait until he flies off, then – but only if you think it's a good idea – you can go that way."

"What if he flies straight up?" Katie teased.

"Easy," said Sally. "We'll throw you after him."

Joanna said nothing.

They waited, but the blackbird seemed fixed to the spot.

Joanna was the one to lose patience first. She clapped her hands and the bird flew off – towards the sea.

Katie started to protest immediately. She wanted a recount.

She was still protesting five minutes later when they breasted the crest of a small hill and stood on the top of the cliffs looking out over the sea. The evening sun, red in a gold and purple sky, was reflected in a million glowing, sparkling mirrors in the water, the motion of the waves making them shimmer and shift like a stream of rubies and gold coins being dripped from a gigantic hand.

Even Katie was silent for a moment, her eyes wide with the beauty of the scene before her, her pert nose breathing in the salty tang of the sea.

Joanna laughed out loud, exhilarated by the freedom of the distant horizon, the sharp smell of ozone lifting her spirits and – inevitably with her – reviving her appetite.

32

Sally was quiet, her eyes moist as she remembered another evening like this. It seemed like a lifetime ago, but was really only two years before. She had been standing on a cliff like this on an evening like this. But then, there had been a hand in each of her hands, one her mother's small cool hand, the other a large, strong, warm hand.

She closed her eyes and it seemed she could feel the rough texture of tweed against her cheek, the unmistakable smell of her father, a mixture of aftershave, the clean sweet scent of his shirts and that other almond smell that was so much his own.

"Something wrong, Sal?" Joanna was looking at her with concern in her black eyes. "You've got tears in your eyes."

Sally shook her head, unable to speak for a moment, then, getting control, tried to laugh. "Must have got something in my eyes." She dabbed at them with her handkerchief.

"I ..." Katie began, but stopped with a yelp as Joanna kicked her on the ankle and glared at her murderously.

Sally dried her eyes, grateful for that strange intuition of Joanna's. In spite of all the kidding about 'Gypsy Joanna', the black-haired girl really did seem able to sense people's moods. Yes, she was scatter-brained, and yes, she did get Sally into some terrible scrapes. But underneath, she was sensitive and understanding. At times, she was a good friend to have.

And Katie, clever and honest, was as loyal to her friends as any bulldog — though not one thousandth part as brave. But she had her own peculiar brand of courage. Frightened or not, she would stick by Joanna and Sally through anything.

Feeling better and brighter, Sally took both her friends by the elbows and laughed. "Forward," she said. "It'll soon be dark and Katie doesn't like the dark." Then, to Joanna, "And if we don't hurry, they might not save supper for us."

They started quickly along the coast road, laughing and giggling, and on the crest of the next hill, across a little bay, they saw the lights of a small village.

"Chertsea," cried Katie. "And it's only another mile."

"I wonder why that old man was so insistent that we go the other way?"

"He didn't like your Lady Muck act, Katie. He wanted to get his own back."

"I wonder ..." Katie looked around her nervously. "Let's hurry. I don't like the feel of this place."

Katie froze.

"There's someone coming," she whispered.

"So what?" Sally was beginning to feel hungry herself. "There's no law says we're the only ones allowed to walk along this path."

"Wait." Joanna clutched Sally's arm. "Let's stay out of sight."

"Now just a minute ..." But at the look in the other girl's eyes, Sally's protest died on her lips, and she simply said, "All right."

Katie didn't argue. In fact, Katie was out of sight behind some bushes first.

A magpie, disturbed by the girls, rose jeering at them and clucking his disapproval lazily soared into the air to circle above them.

Then there was silence broken only by the slow, regular wash of the waves on the pebbles of the beach far beneath them.

34

At first, all they saw was a light dancing and bobbing towards them down the path then, as it came closer, they saw the men behind it.

Sally felt Katie's hand on her arm, gripping it so tightly she had to bite her lips to stop herself from crying out aloud. But as her eyes took in the dreadful sight, all thought of anything but utter horror and repugnance left her.

There were three men.

Faces so white they seemed to glow in the reflection of the lantern one of them carried on a pole, they looked straight ahead, seeming to glide rather than walk along the path in dead, complete silence. Their ragged seamen's clothes from another time were wet and dripping with seaweed. The man with the lantern had one sightless eye and the other men had eyes wide with horror, as if they had seen some unspeakable, terrible sight.

As they passed within ten yards of where the girls were hidden, the stench of rotting seaweed was wafted to them on the soft summer breeze from the sea. In spite of the warmth of the evening, it seemed to carry with it the damp cold of another darker world.

Almost without breathing, the three girls watched as the trio passed by in utter silence.

Suddenly they were gone.

They didn't slowly fade into the distance, they didn't seem to step from the path – they vanished. Completely and instantly, they weren't there any more.

Katie collapsed on the grass sobbing. "I knew we shouldn't have come this way," she repeated over and over.

Sally's knees started to shake, and she had to sit down on the grass to recover herself, her palms moist and the sound of her own blood pounding in her ears. She breathed deeply, evenly, trying to still the mad thumping of her heart.

"No!"

Katie and Sally turned to stare at Joanna, her face pale and her eyes wide. She was shaking her head from side to side and muttering to herself in a daze, "No. They weren't right. I would have known if they were right. They didn't feel right. They didn't feel right."

"Joanna!" Sally called sharply, afraid the other girl was becoming hysterical. "Are you all right?"

Joanna knelt down to bring her face level with Sally's and stared into her eyes. Amazed, Sally saw that Joanna was not afraid. She was annoyed.

"It's a trick, Sal, only a trick. I don't know how they did it, and I don't know why they did it, but I do know that they weren't genuine!"

"They looked real enough to me." Katie's voice was shaky.

Involuntarily, Sally shivered. "And to me. Those faces – and that smell . . ."

"And the cold!" Katie rubbed her face with both hands.

"They weren't real ghosts." Joanna put her hand on Sally's shoulder. "I would have known."

"How?"

"I don't know, but I would have known." She shrugged her shoulders. "I don't know how I would have known, but I would have. Those men were frightening, but that's what they were – men!"

"How did they do it then?" Katie demanded, the prospect of a good argument making her feel better.

"I don't think it's any good looking now, it's too dark,"

said Joanna. "But I'll guarantee if we come back here tomorrow in daylight, we'll find some sort of tracks or some other trace of those three. I'm sure of that!"

Her confidence made Sally feel better, and the fact that Katie wanted to argue with Joanna about the three men seemed to make them seem somehow less frightening.

It was dark now, and the three girls hurried along the cliff path towards the lights that were Chertsea.

"I don't think we should tell anyone," Joanna broke the silence.

"Nor me," Sally agreed.

To their surprise, even Katie fell in with them.

"They'll think it's a story I've made up to frighten them," Joanna said. "So maybe it's better that we come back here tomorrow without telling anyone why."

"Agreed."

"Joanna?" Katie's voice quavered. "Didn't you say something about a ship being wrecked off the coast here?"

"Yes, the *Sally Hanson*."

"Well what's that?" She pointed a shaking finger at a green light on the water.

Sally answered for her. "That, Katie is a light on a boat. It's called a navigation light. See, there's another one and that one's red. By the look of it, it's an electric light. I don't think they had electric lights on ships two hundred years ago."

"Phew!" Katie let out her breath explosively. "That's a relief."

"It's very close inshore, isn't it?" Joanna stared down at the lights below them.

"Probably trawling for flatfish." Sally remembered a

37

deep, well-loved voice saying that in another place in another time. There was a deep gnawing emptiness at the memory.

Whatever explanation accounted for the appearance of the three frightening figures of the seamen, Sally knew that memories of the past could return, like ghosts, to haunt someone.

Ghosts didn't only come in the night, they came at any time, stirred up by a sight or a sound or even a scent. They weren't frightening, either, but the emotions they invoked were harder to bear than fear – the longing, the yearning to have things as they once had been.

She shook her head violently.

It was late, it was dark and she had too much to do getting the other two girls to Chertsea to waste time feeling sorry for herself.

"Come on, you two," she said, much louder than she had intended. "If we're going to get there in time for supper, we'd better get a move on!"

A hand brushed her arm and closed on her elbow. Joanna's grip tightened on her arm and gave her a reassuring little squeeze. It was funny how she always knew.

They were on a downward slope into the village and reached the outskirts in five minutes. There was a row of brightly painted old cottages that looked, even in the deepening gloom, as though they belonged on a picture postcard.

"I wonder where the school is?" Katie mused. "You'd think there would be a shop open where we could ask."

"Why don't we knock on one of these doors and ask there?" suggested Joanna.

"Don't tell me," Sally sighed. "You do it so much better than us, Sally ..."

Katie and Joanna grinned.

Because Sally was going to knock on the door of one of the cottages, there was no big argument about which one it would be. She picked the first one, a pink painted one at the end of the row.

Warily, in case there was a dog, she opened the small, white painted gate and walked up the path, the gravel crunching under her feet. There was a light on in the front room, so she knew there was someone in.

The old iron doorknocker creaked as she raised it, then dropped against the door with a resounding crash.

The light in the front room went off.

She raised the knocker again, ensuring that it only knocked on the door this time, but there was no response.

"Hello," she called softly. "Is there anyone in?" A bolt rattled home in the door. "Is there anyone there?" Even to Sally, the question sounded ridiculous, but she couldn't think of anything else to say. She knocked the knocker again, but there was no response.

"Knock again," Katie called, safely on the other side of the gate.

"There's no point," Sally replied. "Whoever's in there evidently doesn't like visitors."

She crunched down the path and was about to go into the cottage next door when the light went off there, too. Mystified, she looked along the row of cottages and, where before there had been a row of lighted windows, every cottage was in darkness.

"This is ridiculous!" Joanna's voice sounded very loud in the stillness. "There must be someone in."

"There's no law says you have to answer the door at night." Sally started off down the road towards the harbour and the centre of the village. "Maybe there's a cafe or a pub or somewhere open."

But there wasn't. A strange, eerie quiet lay over the entire village with not even the sound of a dog to disturb it.

"What do we do now?" Katie was getting nervous again.

"I don't know." Sally shrugged her shoulders. "I suppose the only thing we can do is look for the school ourselves. We know it's not actually in the village ..."

"Sally!" Katie's whisper was urgent. "There's ... there's something coming ..."

A pale, flickering light was gyrating and dancing towards them, down the hill that led out of the village on the other side. In the still silent air there came a sound, a grumbling, rumbling, rattling sound of metal – like armour – or like chains.

As the light reached the bottom of the hill, bearing down on them inexorably, a figure behind it was outlined against the night sky, a huge black, flapping creature.

Sally tugged at Katie's arm, but the other girl was frozen to the spot, petrified, her eyes wide and staring, her mouth open in a soundless scream.

Unable to move her, Sally turned towards the approaching figure, not knowing what she could do but determined she would not desert her friend. The light bobbed and juddered and shone into Sally's dazzled eyes.

"Hey!" A loud voice assailed them from the darkness. "Stay where you are!"

Sally clenched her fists and prepared to stand her ground.

The light went out.

"Caught you!" The sound was followed by a deep,

rich laugh. "Sally Barnes, Joanna Carter and Katherine Wallace, I presume?"

Now that her eyes were becoming accustomed to the dark, Sally could make out the shape of a face beneath the peaked hat.

"It is you, isn't it? Or have I come across another three young women who just happen to fit the descriptions I've got?" He laughed again and his voice was teasing. "Don't tell me. You've seen the ghosts and been struck dumb?"

"As a matter of fact – " Katie finished on a yelp as Joanna stamped on her foot.

"How did you know our names?" Sally spoke fast and loud to drown out the noises Katie was making.

"Your headmistress, Mrs Hay, sent for me and gave me your descriptions. She's worried sick about you, so we'd best get back up that hill as fast as we can." He started to wheel his bicycle, rattling and bumping back up the cobbles. "Tell you what, girls, if you ever come down that hill on a bike, make sure you're not carrying any milk – you'll turn it into butter. I'm still vibrating." He made his voice wobble and they all laughed. "That's better," he said. "Now why don't you tell me how you got here and what made you so frightened when I came down the hill?"

Sally liked this big, friendly policeman, but there was something that made her hold back the story about what they had seen on the cliff top. It wasn't just that she thought he wouldn't believe her, it was more. She wanted time to think about it, time to make her own mind up about it before she shared it with strangers. Besides, it was something she would have to discuss with the other girls.

41

So she told him about the station at Little Chertsea, the old man's warning not to come along the cliff path, and what had happened when they tried to get an answer at the cottage.

"They're a funny lot in this village," the policeman said. "I've been here six months and they still won't speak to me."

"You're not from round here, then?" Joanna asked.

"Can't you tell from my accent?" he asked.

"It sounds perfectly normal to me."

"That's because I come from London same as you."

"Oh!"

By now, they were at the top of the hill, in front of a big, old building which, unlike the few cottages in the village, had all the lights burning.

"Chertsea Old School. This is your home for the next two weeks."

"Are you coming in?" Sally asked as he held the door open for them.

"No. I've got a couple of calls to make tonight." As they stood in the doorway, he swung a long leg over his bicycle. "You tell Mrs Hay I'll call in tomorrow morning to make sure everything's all right." He started to pedal away, but turned to wave.

The girls waved back.

Then they went in to face the headmistress.

Later as they lay in bed with the lights out, Katie was the one who wanted to talk. "I still don't understand," she said.

"It's quite simple, Katie," Sally whispered. "If Miss Parson hadn't made us go into the other compartment on the train, we wouldn't have got off at the wrong station. Mrs Hay wasn't angry at us, but she was worried sick that something might have happened to us."

42

"And as she said, we're supposed to be on holiday and enjoying ourselves," said Joanna, who hated to be left out of a conversation. "So ..."

"There was no point in punishing us." Sally continued.

"That walk was enough punishment," Joanna groaned. "That and being late for supper."

"I didn't mean that ..."

"Shush," warned Sally.

"Remember our other punishment," whispered Joanna. "That's sharing a room with Alyson."

"What are you three whispering about?" Alyson's tone was petulant. "I'm trying to sleep."

"If we wanted you to know what we were talking about, we wouldn't be whispering." Joanna was the soul of tact. "But if you like, I'll tell you more about the Chertsea ghosts ..."

"I want to go to sleep."

Sally yawned loudly. "So do I."

"And we do want to be up bright and early in the morning." Joanna sounded tired, too.

"Why are you getting up early in the morning?" Alyson was more curious than annoyed now.

Sally knew that Joanna was seriously considering telling Alyson what they has seen on the clifftop – just to ensure she had pleasant dreams – so she quickly said, "We think we know where there's an adder's nest, and we want to get there before people start walking about and frighten it away."

"Yeugh!" Alyson said, and Sally knew she wouldn't have to worry about Alyson following them next morning.

43

Chapter 4

Anger And Sadness

"What time did you say?" Sally rubbed sleep from her eyes and stared at Katie's face in the pale light that filtered through the drawn curtains.

"Quarter to six," Katie whispered. "You did say you wanted to be wakened early."

"It's still the middle of the night!"

"Shush." Joanna was standing on one foot as she tried to struggle into her jeans. "You'll waken horrible Alyson."

Yawning and stretching, Sally sat up in her bed. The idea of exploring the cliffs didn't seem so inviting at this early hour.

"Come on. We want to get up on the cliff before anyone else." Joanna sat on her bed and pulled on her trainers.

"Yes." Katie was pulling a comb through her short mousy hair. "Once this lot start milling about up there, you won't be able to find elephant tracks."

"I guess so." Sally got out of bed. "I don't suppose there's any hot water?"

"No."

"We can have a shower later, when we come back from our swim." Joanna had sorted out her costume and a towel.

"A swim?" Katie was incredulous. "At this time in the morning?"

"Can you think of a better excuse for us to be going out in the middle of the night? Quarter to six! I didn't know there was such a time!"

Alyson turned over in her bed and muttered something in her sleep.

"Maybe we'd better get going." Sally hurried into her clothes and took her toothbrush and comb out to the bathroom.

The water was cold, and the girls were out and on their way to the clifftop in less than ten minutes.

The morning was bright and promised a glorious day, the slight breeze coming off the sea waking them up thoroughly and – as usual – making Joanna hungry.

Carefully they went along the track looking for a sign, any sign, that someone other than themselves had come along that track the night before. There was nothing – nothing that they could see, anyway.

In the mystery books they read, there was always a stray footprint, or a scrap of cloth as a clue, but here, there was nothing.

The girls did find a way down the cliff to the shore below, where the three men had disappeared, but there was no sign that anyone had used it.

"Let's go down," Katie said. "It seems to be a nice beach down there and if we are going to go for a swim, that's as good a place as any."

"All right," Sally agreed. "We'll go down that way, but first, I want to try something."

"What?" asked Katie, eagerly. She was not the sporty type, and would rather have done almost anything than go swimming.

"Go back to those bushes where we hid last night and watch me walk along here. See if I disappear the way those men did."

Both girls went back and crouched down behind the gorse in approximately the place where they had been last night. Once more the magpie rose chattering and grumbling to circle above them before heading inland.

Sally walked along the top path, then, when she came level with the place where the downward path started, dropped down the three feet or so to the first ledge below the clifftop.

"Perfect," Katie said, as she came walking up to where Sally sprawled in the early sunshine. "You just disappeared."

"That shows us how it could be done," Joanna remarked slowly, "but what good is that? It doesn't tell us why anyone would want to frighten us like that."

"Of course," Katie said, nervously looking around her, "they could have been real ghosts."

In the fresh clean morning, with the sparkling sea in front of them and no shadows or mists for spirits to hide in, no one could have believed in the souls of dead sailors haunting a village for over two hundred years.

Not even Joanna.

Laughing, the three friends ran down the path to the clean, crisp sand.

The water was cold and crystal clear, driving any thoughts of dark and brooding spirits out of their minds as they frolicked in the rippling water. Even Katie enjoyed the exercise.

Refreshed and glowing, they dried themselves in the growing warmth of the sun and decided to walk along the beach to the village rather than go back along the clifftop.

They turned over rocks to see tiny crabs scuttle frantically out of the light, splashed in the warming shallow pools caught in depressions in the rocks and skimmed smooth sided pebbles out over the water. They shrieked and giggled, as clouds of sea birds swooped and wheeled above them, competing with their raised voices, screeching and quarrelling.

Before they reached the village, there was a massed jumble of sharp rocks which rose sharply, cutting off the sight of the village ahead of them and stretching out to sea.

They put on their shoes before clambering up and over the rocks, for the edges of the broken slabs were sharp and cruel, and the algae on the crazy angled shards of stone made it treacherous underfoot.

Joanna got to the top of the outcrop first and turned to smile down at them, little Katie making heavy work of the ascent, Sally stopping to look at a fine bunch of mussels festooned along one side of a particularly large piece of rock.

Suddenly, Joanna gave a short sharp gasp. As Sally stared up at her, she seemed to sway, both hands covering her face.

"Joanna!" Sally scrambled nimbly up the rocks, reaching the top as Joanna crumpled into a heap. "Whatever's wrong?"

"I — I don't know." Joanna's face was drawn and white, the fine lines of her cheek bones standing out gaunt and harsh. Her black eyes were large and round, the pupils swollen, and there was a faint sheen of moisture on her cold skin. "It's something – something so sad about this place. No. Not sad, that's not the right word, it's more regret ... waste ... anger. Oh, Sally," her face was frightened. "They're so angry, so angry!" With a little gasp, she shut her eyes and put her hand to her breast. "And there's sadness, too." She shivered violently. "Let's go away from this place, Sally. Let's go away from here right now."

Together, Katie and Sally helped Joanna down the other side of the rocks to the beach where they had to let her sit down, her trembling legs barely able to support her.

"You stay here with her, Sal." Katie's worried face was almost as pale as Joanna's. "I'll go and see if I can get some help."

"Best go up to the school, Katie. I don't think you'll get much help in the village."

"I'll try, anyway," said Katie, trying to smile reassuringly at Joanna. "Maybe I could get her something to eat."

Joanna tried to smile in return, but it was an effort.

Sally kept her arm round Joanna's shoulders, desperately trying to will the warmth from her own body into Joanna's shaking, icy cold frame.

At last Joanna's shivering became less violent, but she was still weak and too tired to walk on her own. However, with Sally's support, she was able to make her way slowly over the round pebbles towards the sandy cove that ran down from the village to the sea.

They sat down to rest on the warm sand, a little colour returning to Joanna's face as Sally rubbed her hands vigorously with a towel.

"Sally, before it goes I've got to tell you ..."

"Don't talk, Joanna, rest."

"But I've got to tell you."

"Sally! Joanna!"

The girls looked round to see Katie and the tall figure of the policeman running towards them over the sand. A huge wave of relief swept over Sally.

"What's all this, young lady?" The big policeman showed his white teeth in a smile as he slipped off his acket and bent over Joanna, but there was no laughter in his eyes as he wrapped the garment round her thin cold shoulders and gently lowered her on to the beach with Sally's rolled up towel as a pillow.

Joanna sighed and her eyes closed.

Gently, but firmly, Sally was edged aside as the policeman felt Joanna's pulse then carefully raised her eyelid to look at her eye.

"She's fainted." He sat back on his heels and turned his head to smile at the two girls. "And me thinking it was something serious!"

As though she weighed nothing, he lifted the unconscious Joanna, still wrapped in his jacket, and carried her easily over the sand to the road that ran along by the beach. "I'll carry her up to the school and we can call a doctor from there, but in the meantime, one of you had better run on ahead and let your headmistress know we're coming. We don't want to frighten everyone to death by just walking in on them like this."

White faced and frightened, Katie nodded her head vigorously, then started up the hill to the school.

When they walked through the village they passed a small, silent group of old women, dressed in dark clothing. Their faces were solemn and fearful, and on not one of them did Sally see a hint of sympathy.

49

Hostile and resentful, the women stepped aside to let the policeman through with his burden.

"I told you they weren't a friendly lot around here." The policeman's face was grim and hard set. "I don't think you and your friend would have got any help from them."

Worried though she was about Joanna, Sally couldn't help noticing that there were only old women in the group. There were no men, no children and no young women, and there was complete silence.

It was a strange unnerving experience.

Joanna gave a little moan and opened her eyes.

"What . . . what happened?"

"Too much excitement, young lady, that's what happened." The eyes crinkled round the corners. "You went swimming too early in the morning and I bet you didn't have any breakfast, either."

"Could you please put me down, constable?" There was colour in Joanna's face now, but it was the red of embarrassment. "I think I can manage to walk."

He laughed and set her down on her feet. "With pleasure, miss. You may look underweight, but on a hill like this, you weigh more than enough."

Joanna was weak, but her legs did support her.

"And for your information, those stripes on the sleeve of that tunic which suits you rather well, mean that I'm a sergeant. Sergeant Harris."

"I want to thank you for your help, Sergeant Harris," Sally smiled hesitantly, "I don't know what I would have done if you hadn't shown up."

"You were coping very well, and I'm sure you would have managed without me," he laughed. "Now, if we don't get up to the school and get the kettle on for some

tea, you might have another fainting fit on your hands –
me!"

With Joanna's arm round her shoulders, Sally turned
into the gate of the school, to be met by a worried Mrs
Hay and a grim faced, disapproving Miss Parson.

"Are you all right, Joanna?" Mrs Hay put her hands
on Joanna's face and stared into her eyes.

"Young girls today," Miss Parson tutted primly, "running wild and ..."

"I think we should get Joanna indoors, Miss Parson."
Mrs Hay interrupted her. For the first time in the three
years that Sally had known her, Mrs Hay was annoyed –
and not with Joanna.

"That's a good idea, Mrs Hay," Sergeant Harris said.
"Then, if this lady here wouldn't mind, I think we could
all do with a nice cup of tea." He smiled at Miss Parson
who simpered. "I understand you not only teach domestic science, but also make a terrific cuppa?"

Miss Parson's face went bright red, and she fluttered
like a newly emerged butterfly. "Yes, certainly, I'll see to
it right away. Excuse me ..." And she bustled away,
suddenly looking very important.

"Do they give lessons in diplomacy in the police force
now?" Mrs Hay laughed while she and Sally got Joanna
into the school.

"No," the sergeant grinned. He winked at Sally. "But
about half of the calls a policeman has to make are on
nice little ladies like Miss Parson."

That wink made Sally feel very grown up. It was the
sort of thing her father used to do, include her in and
make her feel part of the adult world.

They got Joanna, whose colour was now back to normal, into the dining room and seated in a chair.

51

"I've telephoned for a doctor," Mrs Hay told her, "and now I want you to sit there quietly until he gets here. Will you stay with her, Sally, while I have a word with the sergeant here?"

They went out leaving Sally and Joanna alone.

"What happened, Sal?" Joanna was back to normal.

"That's what I wanted to ask you!"

"I don't know!"

"Don't know? You frighten Katie and me half to death and you don't know what happened?"

"One minute I was climbing up the rocks, the next I woke up with that policeman carrying me up the hill and you looking as though you'd just been told you were to spend the next ten years with old Parson."

"Can't you remember all you were babbling about somebody being sad or angry?"

Joanna's face was blank. "Not a thing, Sal. I don't remember anything."

The sergeant came back in and seated himself in a chair opposite Joanna. "Now, Joanna," he said, evidently having found out the girls' names from Mrs Hay, "I want you to tell me exactly what you were doing, and how you came to faint."

Joanna told him about them going swimming, then walking along the beach and climbing up on the rock.

"That's all? You're not holding anything back, are you?"

"I've told you everything, sergeant, from when we first arrived on the beach to when I woke up being carried up the hill."

"Nobody's been filling your head with silly stories about this place, have they?" He had taken his jacket from around Joanna's shoulders and was putting it back

52

on. "I know how you young girls like to frighten each other with ghost stories."

Something dropped from his pocket and he stooped quickly to pick it up, but not before Sally got a good look at the object. It was a large gold-coloured earring – the sort she'd seen in pictures of old time sailors.

"I've . . . I've got a book that mentions the *Sally Hanson*." Joanna said hesitantly.

"Ah!" Sergeant Harris quickly slipped the earring into his pocket. "So you know that the spot where you had your fainting fit is where the *Sally Hanson* grounded?"

"No. I didn't know that."

"Now Sally," the sergeant said to the blonde girl, "I want you to tell me exactly what happened this morning, telling me anything which Joanna missed out."

"I can't tell you a lot more, sergeant. It was just as Joanna described it except that she started to babble a bit before she fainted."

"Did she now?" Sergeant Harris leant forward and looked keenly at Sally. "Tell me what she said."

Chapter 5

A Discovery

The arrival of the doctor saved Sally from further questioning, which was a huge relief. Not that she wanted to keep anything from the friendly, comfortable sergeant, but she would have felt such a fool telling him, on a bright, clear sunny day, about three strange ghostly figures haunting the cliffs at night.

Even to herself, it sounded ridiculous.

She would discuss it with Katie and Joanna then, if they were agreeable, they could tell the friendly sergeant the whole story.

The thought of that gold earring in his pocket made Sally think that he knew part of the tale already.

The doctor told Mrs Hay that Joanna was to be kept quiet and out of the sun for a few days, but apart from the fact that she had caught a slight chill, he did not think there was anything wrong with her.

So, that afternoon, while the rest of the girls went on a trip to a nearby Saxon church, Joanna, with Sally and Katie to keep her company, stayed behind with Miss Parson who was determined they should get into no more trouble.

They had become bored with Scrabble and were sitting in the room they shared, Joanna longing to get out in the sunshine. Sally and Katie trying to convince her that the sunshine would be just as warm and just as enticing in two days' time when she was allowed out in it again.

"I feel like a prisoner!" Joanna listlessly turned over the pages of a magazine. "And what's worse is that I'm making you two prisoners as well. If it wasn't for me, you ..."

"Could be tramping round some boring old church with horrible Alyson telling us that her parents went round one twice as old wherever they went on holiday last year." Katie pulled a face. "If I'm going to be bored, I'd rather it was with you two."

"Can we be serious for a moment, girls?" Sally got out a note book and pencil. "A lot's happened to us in the past day, and I think we've got to decide what to do."

"You're not thinking of telling anyone what we saw on the cliffs, are you?" Katie looked alarmed. "They'll think we're making a joke."

"Or they'll think we're some kind of loonies." Joanna went over to the window and looked out. "I mean, look at it out there. Bright sunshine and spooks don't go together."

"I don't know," Sally said doubtfully. "I'm beginning to think we should tell that policeman what we saw."

"Have you got a crush on him, Sal?" Joanna peered into her face. "You go very quiet – and all sort of gooey – whenever he's around."

"And he's old enough to be your father!" Katie said, without thinking. Then realising her words may have upset Sally, she took off her spectacles and polished them vigorously, as she always did when she was embarrassed.

"Don't be so silly, either of you!" But Sally's face was scarlet and her cheeks were hot. "He's a nice man and he tries to treat us as though we were grown up, that's why I like him, and that's why I don't want to keep any secrets from him."

"D'you think he'll still treat us as grown up if we tell him we saw not one – but three ghosts – out for a walk?" Katie had nearly rubbed the lenses away by now.

"I think he knows something he's not telling us." Sally told them about the gold earring.

"So you think he thinks the same as us, that there's someone trying to make people think there are ghosts in Chertsea?" Katie was twiddling her thumbs now. It was something that drove the other two up the wall, but they knew it was the only way she could think properly. "How do you explain Joanna's queer turn down on the beach?"

"I can't. How about you, Joanna?"

The dark-haired girl's face furrowed in a frown. "I've tried and tried to remember, but the whole thing's just a blank. What was it I said to you, Sally? Just before Katie arrived with reinforcements?"

"I can't remember exactly," Sally frowned. "I was too worried about you to pay much attention, but it was something about you had to tell me then, before it – whatever it is – went."

"And as usual, you wouldn't let me talk."

"That's hardly fair, Joanna. I was worried about you."

There was a quiet tap on the door, then it swung open.

"Sally," Miss Parson was back to normal, prim and grim. "I'm going to write some letters and I find I'm short of stamps. Would you go down into the village and get me some?" She cracked her face into the briefest of smiles. "I would go myself, but I did promise the head-mistress that I would stay here and look after Joanna."

"Is there a post office in the village?" Sally hadn't seen any sign of shops in her brief glimpses of Chertsea.

"There's a general store, and I believe they sell stamps there. It's on the other side of the village, near the old harbour."

"I'll go with her," Katie said, eager to get out in the sunshine.

"No," Miss Parson was very firm. "You will stay here where I can keep an eye on you. If Miss Barnes goes on her own, I can trust her to come back."

All the signs of another lecture were there, so Sally very quickly agreed that she would go, and took the money from Miss Parson.

On a sudden impulse, Sally decided to take her camera with her.

Once again, she was struck by the silence in the tiny village, by the absence of children and dogs. It looked pretty enough with the cottages painted in pastel colours and the quaint cobbled streets but, in spite of the bright sunshine, there was an air of desolation about the place, as though it wasn't really lived in.

She found the general store by the harbour, an old fashioned shop which looked as though it would stock everything from clothes pegs to firelighters.

There were three women in the shop, but when Sally walked in, her entrance heralded by the tinkling of the bell above the door, they fell silent, turning their hostile gazes on her.

Behind the counter, was an old, wrinkled man.

"Do you sell postage stamps?" asked Sally.

The man nodded, not speaking.

"I'd like half a dozen first class stamps, please."

Silently, he took a folder from under the counter and tore off her six stamps, thrusting them across the counter at her.

Sally paid him the money and waited for the change, uncomfortably aware of three pairs of eyes focused on her back.

"Thank you." She scooped up the coins he put on the counter and thrust them into her pocket then, as she turned and caught the eyes of one of the women on her, she smiled and said, "Nice day, isn't it?"

There was a flash of fear in the woman's eyes before she turned away from Sally and pretended to look at the display of ancient tins of baked beans piled high on the counter.

Annoyed now, Sally put on her brightest smile and turned back to the shopkeeper. "Have you any post-cards of Chertsea?" she asked. "I want to send some to my friends and tell them what a friendly place this is."

Sullenly, the old man behind the counter pointed to a display of picture postcards on a rack by the door, and Sally went over to them, pretending to study them with interest.

She nearly screamed when a hand reached out and plucked timidly at her sleeve. It was the woman she had spoken to, but now there was a different expression in her eyes. "Are you the girl that was with that poor lass who fainted on the beach this morning?"

"Yes."

There was a soft murmur from the other two women, and the woman who was talking to Sally glanced defiantly at them before continuing. "Is she all right?"

"Yes, thank you." Sally stared at the woman's face, old and wrinkled and drawn with strain. "She's got to stay out of the sun for a few days, that's all."

The old woman put her wrinkled hand on the door-handle and turned it. "I'll walk a way with you back up to the school," she said, and there was more murmuring from the other two women. "We don't see a lot of young folk here, and it'll be nice to talk to someone from outside."

Reaching the bright sunshine of the street, the old lady clutched at Sally's arm and gently led her towards the old fashioned quay, away from the shop.

As they walked slowly across the worn mossy cobbles, the huddled figure of the old lady, kept looking round, as though afraid of being overheard, and Sally found herself doing the same.

"Listen, lass," the cracked old voice hissed fiercely, "we don't have a lot of time, so listen well."

Sally nodded her head vigorously.

"You and those other girls up at the school, keep away from the coast road tonight. I can't explain why, but for your own good you stay away from it – and keep those other girls away from it, too."

Her fingers hooked into Sally's arm and squeezed it tightly.

"But why?" asked Sally.

"Granny!" Sally looked round as a young man dressed like a fisherman came out of the general store and hurried over the cobbles towards them. "So that's where you are!" His teeth showed white against his swarthy skin as he put out a hand and took the old woman by the arm.

"I hope she hasn't been a nuisance to you, miss." He

59

smiled at Sally and firmly drew the old woman away from her. "She's getting very old, and you know how old people go sometimes." With his other hand, he tapped his forehead significantly.

For the briefest of instants, the old woman's hand closed on Sally's arm once more and she felt the gnarled fingers dig into her flesh.

"Now, come on, Granny. Let's get you home," said the young man.

Sally looked into the old woman's face and saw despair.

"We've just been having a nice chat," Sally said brightly. "I was asking about what Chertsea was like in the old days."

"Well, mayhap you can finish your chat some other time, but Granny's got to go for her nap now." He was very firm, as he tucked the woman's arm under his and started to lead her away. "When she gets tired, she sometimes starts to ramble."

"Maybe I can walk along with you," Sally smiled, "I'm not going anywhere in particular."

The smile faded from the man's face and his deep voice took on a different tone. "Strangers get her too excited, miss." There was a hard look in his green eyes. "Especially strangers who get too curious."

Sally let her smile fade, too. "Perhaps there's something going on here that strangers should be curious about?"

"That's possible." The man dropped all pretence of politeness. "But if those strangers don't take warnings to mind their own business, then they deserve all that's coming to them!"

He turned his back on her and started to walk away, almost dragging the woman with him back to the general

60

store. The door was opened from inside and the two vanished into the dim interior.

Then a hand appeared in the glass panel that comprised the upper half of the door and the 'open' sign was turned to 'closed'.

Sally wandered on to the old quay and sat on a bollard, staring out over the bright, sparkling sea, clean and clear, in the hot sunshine.

This was not the first time she had been warned to stay away from the coast road. The peculiar old station-master at Little Chertsea had told all three girls not to go by the coast road the night before. Then there had been the three figures they had seen on the road, but surely that had been someone trying to frighten them away? And one of the men had had a white-socketed, sightless eye – like the strange man, the man with the ghastly face, she had seen in the store room at the station! He must have been one of them!

But why? And why had that old woman – so obviously afraid – gone out of her way to warn Sally to keep the other girls away from the road that night?

It had to be something illegal. It had to be something to do with the sea – and on a remote part of the coastline like this, it was more than likely to be smuggling.

And if it was, the whole village must be mixed up in it. That was why they were so sullen and so unwilling to talk to strangers.

Idly, Sally let her eyes wander over the boats in the harbour. They looked as though they had been left here to die, their paintwork blistered, their ironwork rusted, all of them lying very low in the water as though they had already started to sink.

None of them looked as though they could make it out of the harbour, never mind out to sea.

Then her eye was taken by a clean, new-looking rope tied to a bollard further down the quay. It looked out of place amongst the decaying crates and rotting fishing nets which were abandoned in an untidy jumble down to the outer wall of the harbour.

Because the tide was low, whatever was moored there was out of the line of Sally's sight. Trying to appear casual, in case she was being watched from the shop, Sally got to her feet then, whistling and walking with her hands behind her back, she ambled along the quay to a position from which she could look down and see what was there.

Sally saw a long, low shape covered by a tarpaulin. From the outline, it looked like a high speed motor launch with another smaller tarpaulin-covered shape in tow. That must be a dinghy. The new rubber tyres which had been secured to the algae covered stone of the quay as bumpers were black and new. The iron ladder which ran down the side of the quay to the boat showed signs of use, the rust which covered the rest of the ladder being worn through on the treads.

The girl looked round her to make sure that there was no one who could see her, then she made her way down the ladder and stepped onto the craft hidden beneath the tarpaulin cover.

Sally lifted up the covering. Before her was an expensive-looking motor launch. Although she knew little about boats, it was obvious to her that this craft had no business being in a decayed, deserted quayside.

Leaving the cover pulled back, Sally took some photographs of the launch. She would show the pictures to Sergeant Harris. He would know what the mystery was all about.

Putting the cover back in place, Sally hurried her way up the ladder, and stood once again on the quayside.

"So you couldn't take a warning, eh?"

Sally's heart leapt with fright as she turned quickly to see that the young man who had taken the old woman away, was standing behind her. His arms were folded across his chest and he was balanced lightly on the balls of his feet, poised and alert. "I knew the copper wasn't around in the village so I took a chance and left the boat out here. Didn't expect any kids to come in nosing around." The man shook his head in mock sadness. "Now what am I going to do with you?"

"Do with me?" Sally echoed, her eyes flickering round wildly for a way of escape.

"Well, now you know it all, I can hardly let you go, can I?" It was as though he was trying to appear reasonable.

"I – I don't know what you're talking about," Sally protested. "I don't know anything ..."

"Come on, girl, give me credit for not being entirely stupid. Here you are poking around and you find a brand new launch obviously hidden here. You know how isolated this village is, you've been warned to stay away from the coast road at night – and you don't know what's going on?"

"What – what do you mean?"

"It's obvious, isn't it? We've got a cargo of smuggled goods coming in tonight, so I've got to keep you out of the way until we've done our little bit of business ..." He moved to cut off Sally's path back along the quay.

"Please let me go. I won't tell anyone."

"Not even that nosey copper you're getting so friendly with? Pull the other one, it's got bells on it."

"I'll scream!"

"Go ahead," he laughed. "See how much good that'll do you." He pointed at the ladder leading down to the motor launch. "The one thing screaming will do is annoy me – and I'm not a nice person when I'm annoyed. So you just get down that ladder quietly, and nobody's going to hurt you."

"What – what are you going to do?"

"I'm going to take you on a little cruise out to sea."

Sally looked at his broad shoulders and the hard lines of his face. It would be madness to even think of resisting. This man was young and fit – and ruthless. If she pretended to give in to him now, there was at least a chance she could make an attempt to get free later, when he wasn't expecting it as he obviously was now.

She was frightened – very frightened – but her mind was working.

She let her shoulders slump as though in despair and meekly climbed down the ladder on to the shrouded deck of the launch.

The man jumped down lightly beside her and expertly undid the knot that held the tarpaulin down over the cabin of the launch. Folding it back, he uncovered a door which he opened.

"Down there." He pointed inside.

Silently, Sally climbed down the short stairway that led to a surprisingly spacious cabin. In the light from the open door, she could see that it was well appointed, looking for all the world like one of the luxury show rooms she'd seen at exhibitions. The floor was carpeted and there were couches along either side of the cabin which looked as though they would fold down into beds.

"You'll be quite comfortable here," the man said, as he, too, came down the ladder. "Unfortunately, I'm going to have my hands full taking the launch out to sea, so I'm going to have to tie you up for a little while. It won't be for long." He put his hand on her shoulder and made her sit down on one of the couches. "Now, before I tie you up, is there anything you want?" He opened one of the cupboards and took out a length of twine. "A fruit juice? The use of the bathroom? That's it through there." He pointed at one of two doors at the other end of the cabin.

Sally shook her head and the man expertly looped the twine round both her wrists and secured them. "Not too tight?" he asked.

She shook her head.

"I'm going up on deck now, and I want you to stay here quietly and not do anything silly. Got that?" He gave her bonds a final tug to ensure she was securely fastened.

"Please," Sally pleaded. "Please let me go."

"Too late now, girl. You should have taken our warnings and kept your nose out of things which don't concern you."

"You'll never get away with this, you know." Sally was defiant. "If I don't get back to the school soon, they'll start to look for me."

"And they won't find you." He laughed nastily. "Just another girl who wouldn't do what she was told. Wandered off and got lost."

"That woman back in the village saw me."

"She won't talk." He got to his feet and walked over to the short flight of stairs that led up to the deck. "She's got too much to lose."

"You can't keep a whole village quiet – and they can't all be in on smuggling."

"I don't think you realise the size of the operation you've stumbled on," he grinned unpleasantly. "We don't leave things to chance."

"What do you mean?"

"We've got three old men from the village tucked safely away. Those people back there know that if they don't cooperate – all the way – they won't see their old grandfathers again."

A cold chill ran down Sally's spine.

The man's green eyes were cold and merciless. "Let's hope you never have to test us, girl. Let's sincerely hope it never comes to that."

He went up the stairs and closed the cabin door behind him, then, as he replaced the tarpaulin over it, the cabin was plunged once more into darkness.

Chapter 6

No Escape

In the dark, Sally struggled with her bonds, but even her teeth made no impression on the tough, closely woven strands. All her straining and pulling only made the bonds tighter, cruelly cutting into her skin.

She lay back on the couch, her mind racing as she heard the man moving about on the deck above her, preparing to take the craft out to sea. Once they were at sea, there was no place for her to run to, even if she did get her hands loose.

The motion of the boat altered as the powerful engines started up, their deep throb vibrating through the hull, the idle bobbing of a craft at anchor changing to the more purposeful thrust of a craft cleaving its way through water as the engines increased their power and the launch got under way out to sea.

It would have been easy for Sally to give up then. Despair lurked at the corners of her mind waiting to invade her whole mind the moment she surrendered.

Somewhere in the deepest recesses of her memory there was a faint echo of a loved voice saying, "The only time you're beaten is when you admit it ..."

Well, she wasn't beaten yet! Not by a long chalk.

The cabin was flooded with light as the tarpaulin over it was thrown back. When her eyes had adjusted to the brightness, Sally could see the man on deck, through one of the portholes, as he carefully rolled up the tarpaulin then tied it down along the rail of the boat.

He looked up and saw her watching him through the window, and his swarthy face creased into a frown.

The motion of the launch through the water was hypnotic, with its regular thudding as it skidded across the top of the ripples on the sea, up and down, up and down.

Sally felt her eyelids start to close, but fought them open again. Tempting though the thought of sleep was, she needed to stay awake and aware, ready to take any chance, however slight, to escape.

Her eyes wandered round the cabin, looking for something that would help her, but there was nothing. Her gaze stopped at the two doors that led off the cabin.

That man had said something about a bathroom. But there were two doors. Did the other one lead to a kitchen – a galley? If there was a kitchen, there had to be knives. She stood shakily erect, the motion of the boat, and the fact that her hands were tied together made balancing awkward, but Sally persevered and staggered over to the two doors.

The first one she opened led into a tiny bathroom with a shower stall and a handbasin as well as a W.C.

The second led into the tiny galley, pots and pans hooked on to the walls, the drawers on the little sink unit fastened shut with hooks and eyes.

Quickly Sally fumbled open one of the drawers, sighing with gratitude when she discovered it contained cutlery. She fished out a sharp-looking knife and wedged the handle in the opening of the drawer, closing it with her knee to jam the handle so that the blade pointed into the air, the edge towards her.

"Clever girl."

The voice froze Sally in the act of sawing at her bonds. "Pity, though, that you didn't think of it sooner, before I came below," said the man as he took her arms and pulled her back into the cabin and made her sit once more on the couch.

"Virtue is its own reward, you see." He started to untie her wrists. "If I hadn't decided you could do with a breath of fresh air and come down here to fetch you up on deck, you might have got your hands loose – like that!" He pulled the cord and it fell from her wrists.

"What then, though?" he asked as Sally rubbed her numbed wrists to get the blood going again. "If you had been free, would you have hidden behind the door and hit me over the head with a frying pan when I came down?"

"I would have thought of something," Sally defied him. "Somehow, some way I'd have got away."

"And what then? Do you know how to sail one of these things? Or maybe you're a long distance swimmer and think you could manage the three or four miles back to shore?" He nodded his head towards the ladder.

"Get up on deck now, where I can keep an eye on you. You better get used to the idea that there's no escape!"

Obediently, Sally climbed the ladder, her mind a ferment as she rehearsed a dozen plans in her mind and rejected them one by one. No matter what she thought of, it always boiled down to one brutal fact.

This man was young and he was strong and he wasn't stupid.

69

No matter what she did, as long as she was aboard this launch he could find her and overpower her. She had to be realistic about that. And so far, he hadn't been cruel, but if she gave him trouble, there was no telling how nasty he might turn.

But she wasn't going to give up.

On deck, the wind snatched at her long, blonde hair and whipped her cheeks to a bright red. The nose of the launch was out of the water, the hull cleaving the waves and throwing a high, white wake out to either side. Now the tarpaulin had been removed, Sally could see the clean, modern lines of the craft, built for speed. It was easy to see why the boat had had to be covered up back in Chertsea harbour.

She breathed deeply of the sea air, her eyes busy looking everywhere for a way to escape or even a place to hide. But the clean deck was uncluttered, even the dinghy being towed behind, bobbing and bucking in the wake of the power boat.

"In here!" The man put his hand on Sally's shoulder and pushed her into the enclosed bridge. "It's quieter."

Out of the wind, Sally looked down at the bewildering array of instruments and controls and knew that, even if she could get the chance, there was no way she could steer the boat or even stop it.

"Impressive, eh?" The man laughed at her, as though he was showing a guest around his proud possession. "There's nothing in this part of the country could touch her." Lovingly, his hand caressed the wheel. "We can outrun anything in the water in this little beauty."

"Where are we going?" Sally was wondering how long it could be before Miss Parson became alarmed at her absence.

"Not far. There's a trawler lying about five miles off the coast. She should be coming in sight soon ..." He bent over the radar scanner and frowned. "There shouldn't be any other traffic in this area." He adjusted the controls, and the nose of the launch lowered in the water as the craft slowed down. "I think you'd best go below again." He took her by the elbow and started to lead her back to the door of the cabin.

It was now or never. Sally knew she wouldn't have another chance to get free. As they came level with the cabin door, she tripped, and sprawled full length on the deck.

"Come on!" He tugged at her arm, trying to pull her to her feet.

"I – I can't," Sally gasped. "I can't put any weight on my ankle. I think I've sprained it."

"Crawl then! I don't want you on deck if we're going to meet any other shipping."

"I'll try." Sally got on to her hands and knees and laboriously started to move along the deck towards the cabin door. "But I don't think I'll be able to get down the ladder."

"You'll get down if I have to carry you down!" His face was cold and hard and his voice was like a whiplash. "And if this is some kind of a trick ..." He didn't finish the sentence, but the look of menace in his flinty green eyes made Sally shudder.

Supporting herself on the rail, she struggled to stand on one foot as the man anxiously scanned the horizon. "If you could go down and catch me," Sally pleaded.

Muttering, the man swung himself down the ladder, holding on with one hand while he held the other up to Sally.

71

The girl flung herself against the door, slamming it shut and dropping the heavy catch into place to hold it locked. There was a yell and a crash from inside, but Sally hardly noticed as she ran back to the bridge. She knew the door wouldn't hold the man for any length of time, so she would have to act quickly.

She closed her hand on the lever the man had eased back to slow the craft down. She pulled it all the way back with all of her strength, staggering as the engines cut and the bow of the launch dipped into the water sharply, slowing it down as fast as any brake.

The loud hammering from behind her reminded her that she had only minutes before the man freed himself.

There was no sign of any other craft on the horizon. Sally stepped over the boat's rail and poised herself to dive overboard. She plunged into the sea, as a rasping, splintering smash told her the man had broken through the door.

The cold, green water closed over her head, and Sally struck out underwater for the stern of the boat which, propelled by its own momentum, still moved through the water, faster than Sally had expected. When she grasped the side of the dinghy, the jerk as it pulled her arm surprised her so much, she nearly let go again. She managed to hold on and hoist herself over the gunwale and burrow under the canvas that enveloped the dinghy.

She lay huddled up, wet and uncomfortable, knowing that if she wasn't discovered in the next few minutes, she would be safe for a time.

Safe! She almost laughed when she thought about it. Miles out to sea in a small boat, wet and cold with nothing to eat or drink, and she had called it safe.

The boat rocked gently in the light waves, the only

sound the slap of water against the hull. From the motion of the boat, she knew that the launch had not got under way again and she wondered what the man was doing. If he'd seen her go over the side, he probably wouldn't bother searching the launch. She'd gone off the front of the launch so that he wouldn't see she was trying to reach the dinghy, but he wasn't a stupid man, and it might occur to him that she would think it a safe hiding place.

She held her breath and her heart almost stopped beating as the dinghy gave a sudden jerk and she felt it being pulled through the water, jerking and bobbing, as though the man was hauling in the rope that held it, hand over hand.

There was a thump as the side of the dinghy came against the side of the launch and Sally almost screamed aloud as something pointed pressed down the canvas, centimetres from her head. She heard a snapping sound as though someone were plucking at the canvas to see that it was still bound securely round the dinghy, then there was silence.

In spite of the fact that she was cold and damp, Sally felt beads of perspiration on her forehead.

Her heart was beating so loudly she was sure that anyone outside must hear it. Then there was another gentle bump and she felt the dinghy dip down on one side as though someone had stepped aboard it.

There was a blinding rush of light as the canvas was raised towards the bow, then darkness as it was lowered again. Surely he must hear the pounding of her blood in her veins!

The dinghy dipped once more and levelled itself, bobbing quietly and docilely in the light sea.

73

Sally began to breathe again.

She jumped as the engines roared smoothly into life and the dinghy started to move through the water, dancing in the wake of the powerful launch.

The hot sun beating down on the canvas heated her dark hiding place intolerably and the regular movement of the dinghy over the waves was as soothing as the rocking of a cradle.

Cautiously, Sally took off her sneakers and socks and stretched herself full length on the bottom of the small craft, hoping her clothes would dry on her and regretting the fact that when she was in the general stores she hadn't taken the opportunity to buy some chocolate.

The heat and the regular movement, the lack of air and sheer exhaustion were having the inevitable effect on Sally, and her eyelids began to droop.

She had to think of what she was going to do next. She couldn't afford to go to sleep. Sally struggled to get her thoughts in order, to make some sort of plan.

She would have to get word to Sergeant Harris and tell him about the crook's plan for that night.

Desperately she fought to keep control of her thoughts, trying to picture the policeman's face. But his face gave way to another, a face that was never far from her thoughts, the face of her dead father.

He smiled at her and reached out a hand to her.

"You're not going to give up, Sally, are you?"

"No, Dad," she breathed in the darkness. "No."

Then, with the faintest of smiles on her lips, her eyes closed, and she slept.

Chapter 7

No Honour Amongst Thieves

Sally wakened suddenly to silence.

She woke with her mouth dry and her heart pounding furiously, wondering where she was and why it was so dark. Then, as memory flooded back, she felt the sharp, bitter taste of despair.

The motion of the dinghy was from side to side as if it had lost its sense of direction and become once more a plaything at the mercy of the waves. The sound of the launch's motors had gone, so Sally knew they had reached their destination.

"Bring her alongside!" The voice was distorted as though by a loud hailer. "Then get yourself aboard here. You and I have things to talk about!"

There was the scraping of wood against rubber and the rattle of metal. Stifling her breathing, Sally listened intently, hearing the sound of footsteps, the scuffing of a rope being drawn across wood.

The motion of the dinghy lessened subtly, as though it was now being sheltered from the waves. She turned cautiously on her stomach, and carefully inched her way towards the gunwale of the dinghy. Using her fingertips she raised the canvas cover, centimetre by agonising centimetre until she could look out.

The brightness of the day dazzled her at first and it was some seconds before her eyes adjusted enough for her to be able to see. The launch was moored alongside a rusty old trawler. Two ropes were attached to the rusty iron ladder that ran down the hull of the trawler securing the launch by her stern and her bow against a buffer of old tyres which prevented the two vessels from rubbing together. The dinghy in which Sally was hiding bobbed in the lee of the trawler.

The man who had been aboard the launch was climbing the ladder towards the deck where another man waited to meet him. Against the glare of the blue sky, Sally strained her eyes to try and see him clearly.

He was a fat man wearing a once white shirt and light trousers. On his head he wore a crumpled seaman's cap. His unshaven face was scowling, and when he spoke, his accent was not English. In his right hand he held a loud hailer.

"What is this you tell me on the radio about a girl on board?" The fat man pointed the loud hailer at the launch. "You make sure she not on there any more?"

"I made sure."

"Dinghy. What about dinghy?"

"I checked that as well, Dietrich. The girl must have gone to the bottom like a stone."

"Maybe best thing, I think." Dietrich scratched his unshaven jowls. "Save us lot of trouble." He chuckled harshly. "Boss man no like it, Tony. I think you maybe got big trouble."

"Is he aboard?"

"Yes. He say he want to see you as soon as you get here." Dietrich grinned nastily. "You always tell me I'm dumb, Tony. Now we'll see who is dumb."

"Come on," Tony scowled. "Let's get it over with."

The two men walked away across the deck and as they went, their voices faded. Sally dropped the canvas and wriggled over to the other side of the dinghy, cautiously peering out from under the canvas in the direction away from the trawler, the direction, she reasoned, in which land would lie.

There was nothing but sea.

Her only hope now was that Tony would make the return trip to Chertsea without checking the dinghy further.

Approaching voices made Sally drop the canvas hastily and squirm back to the centre of the dinghy.

"I'll be coming with you this trip, so there had better be no further hitches." It was a different voice and a different accent.

"You've never come ashore with me before. Why this time?" Tony's voice was angry. "Don't you trust me any more?"

"This time is different. I have to see my buyers."

"But . . ."

"No buts, Tony. Let's just say that it would be – inconvenient – for me to have my passport examined too closely . . ."

"How are you going to get back? This is supposed to be my last trip – out or in."

"You're going to bring me. It will be your last trip when you've brought me back." There was something about the way he spoke that made Sally sure he was accustomed to giving orders.

77

"Our agreement was that this was my last trip!" Tony was almost shouting. "I take the stuff off from here and deliver it, then I'm through!"

"Tony, Tony, Tony, calm down. I'll pay you to make this one other trip – a lot of money." The man laughed. "You haven't done so badly out of us, have you? You've got this beautiful launch and more money than you'd make from a hundred years of fishing. Now I'm giving you the chance to make even more, just for a little favour."

"A lot of good this boat and the money are going to do me if I'm serving twenty years inside."

"Don't be so nervous, Tony. The whole operation has gone as smooth as silk so far. There's no reason to think anything's going to go wrong now."

"No? We've got that nosey copper poking around and asking questions – and there's those kids up at the old school."

"The policeman isn't going to learn anything, is he? None of those old women in the village are going to talk as long as we've got these three old grandads aboard here. They're a guarantee of good behaviour. You told me so yourself."

Sally's heart beat faster. Now she knew where they were keeping the three men from the village. If only she could get word to the police!

"What about the kids up at the school? How do we guarantee that more of them don't get curious?" asked Tony.

"How is it you say in England? Put the frighteners on them."

"We tried that already and look where it got us. One of them's at the bottom of the sea."

"Well, she's not going to be any more trouble to you," said the man, with a cruel laugh.

Sally's blood ran cold. If a man could laugh at someone drowning, what would he do if he discovered a girl was listening to all he said?

"That's another thing." Tony's voice was tight. "What if anyone saw me take her aboard the launch?"

"It was an accident. You said so on the radio."

"With my record, who's going to believe I didn't help her over the side?"

"Maybe that's a good reason for you to cooperate about this one last trip, Tony!" The voice was menacing.

"I hope you don't mean what I think you mean, Ahmed."

"My friend, would I let you down? Would I – how do you say it? – grass on you?"

"It wouldn't be a good idea, Ahmed. If they get me, I won't go inside on my own."

"Now you're threatening me, Tony. There's no reason for us to fall out, is there? You make this last extra trip for me and I'll see you all right, OK? Now let's get you loaded up."

"All right."

"You go below and get things ready. Oh, and send Dietrich up. I want to talk to him."

There was the sound of retreating footsteps across the deck, then silence.

Sally stifled her sigh of relief. They were going back to Chertsea. She fumbled about with her hand on the bottom of the dinghy. Now she wouldn't have to even consider rowing back to land. She wouldn't have to find the oars.

There were footsteps again on the deck and the

muffled sound of voices Sally had to strain her ears to hear what the men were saying.

"You know what you have to do when we come back, Dietrich?"

"Yes, Mr Rashid. It'll be a pleasure to get rid of him."

"I think it will round the operation off nicely. After tonight we won't need him. After all, he is the only one who's actually seen me." He chuckled evilly. "And we can't afford to give expensive launches like this away."

"No, Mr Rashid." Dietrich's voice was gloating. "And he's going to find out who the dumb one is after all."

Sally shivered in spite of the heat under the canvas. There was perspiration on her forehead, but it was cold and clammy. Her head ached and her legs were stiff and cramped. It was like a bad dream, and the men's words only made it seem more like some evil nightmare.

The noise of scuffling and banging made her tense herself once more.

"Right, Tony." Dietrich sounded almost jovial. "Drop them here. You go down the ladder and I'll pass them down to you."

Suddenly the dinghy was jerked through the water until, with a bump it came up against something solid.

Panic gripped Sally. The dinghy dipped sharply when someone stepped into it and the canvas was ripped back and bright sunlight fell full on her.

Chapter 8

Billy Briggs

"So you searched the dinghy, did you?"

Sally, half conscious, struggled listlessly in Dietrich's powerful grip as Ahmed shouted furiously at Tony. "So she's at the bottom of the sea, eh?"

"Ahmed, I tell you I did search the dinghy."

"What do I do with her?" Dietrich jerked Sally roughly to her feet, but her legs would hardly take her weight and she slumped once more in his grasp.

"What do you think we should do with her, Tony? Maybe you want to take her back to Chertsea with you?" Ahmed put a beautifully manicured hand under Sally's chin and lifted her face.

"Don't be so stupid!"

Blood drained from Ahmed's face at Tony's words, but he controlled himself with a visible effort.

Tony was too angry to notice. "I knew you were going to use the dinghy, didn't I? You think I'd be daft enough to try and hide her there?"

"I put her over the side now, ja?" Dietrich dragged Sally towards the rail of the trawler. She was too weak and dazed to resist.

"No!" Tony's eyes were hard and vicious. "I've got a better idea."

"She's seen me now." Ahmed glared at Tony. "You can't let her go." He nodded at the fat German. "All right, Dietrich."

"Wait." Tony stepped between the rail and Dietrich. "This might work out better for me. If anyone saw her come aboard the launch and then she's found drowned, I'm in trouble." His cold eyes fixed on the other men. "And if I'm in trouble, we're all in trouble."

"So what do you propose?"

Sally was having difficulty keeping her eyes focused and the men's voices were fading and echoing as in a nightmare.

"Look at her. She's got some sort of fever. She's hardly conscious."

"So?"

"If she's reported missing back in Chertsea, they're going to organise a search for her, and that's one thing we can do without, tonight of all nights." Sally fought to concentrate on what he was saying. "But if a trawler were to radio a report that a girl was spotted well out at sea in a sinking boat ..."

The voice faded and Sally slumped to the deck.

Vaguely, as though it was happening to someone else, she was aware of being dragged across the deck, her bare feet catching painfully on the rough planking.

Succeeding waves of mist engulfed her, then let her surface briefly before engulfing her once more.

The sun was shining down onto her face and she was lying in the bottom of a small boat among a tangle of ropes and canvas and wooden struts. Her back was cold and wet and she knew she was lying in water.

"Make it look like an accident." Tony's words penetrated the fog in her brain. "Young girl goes for a trip in a boat, gets washed out to sea, loses the oars ..."

"What if she does make it back to land?" Ahmed's voice came from a distance.

"From way out here?" Tony scoffed. "I know this coast and I know these currents. An experienced seaman would have a hard time to make it back in this old tub – but a semi-conscious girl? No way. If it'll make your mind any easier, we'll take out the bung. That'll give her about forty minutes before she sinks."

"I still think we should take the sail out."

"No need. It'll probably fall to pieces the first time someone touches it. We'll get rid of the oars and I'll tow it further out to sea and leave it."

"You've taken the name off? There's no way it can be traced back to us?"

"Ja." That was Dietrich. "Paint so old it flaked off."

"Pity you can't put the three old men in it with her," Ahmed laughed.

"They're our insurance with the villagers. It's a chance we can't take."

"I still don't like it," Ahmed said.

"I don't know what you're worrying about."

Sally forced her eyes open and saw that Tony was standing over her in the small boat. He said, "It's my neck that's on the line. You won't even be in the country after tonight, and nobody except me's seen you." He kicked at the soggy jumble of old canvas swilling around in the bottom of the boat. "I'm the one that's taking all the risks."

"All right. You tow her out and we'll load up the other dinghy."

83

Sally's eyes fluttered and she sank into a deep, black pit, swirling and spiralling downwards, drowning in darkness.

Dimly, deep down in her mind, she heard that familiar voice saying, "Hold on, Sally, hold on. The only time you're beaten is when you admit you're beaten."

"I am beaten," she cried in her dreams. "I am beaten. There's no way out for me."

Her father's well-remembered face swam into her mind, smiling ruefully the way he used to.

"No, you're not, Sally. My girl doesn't give up that easily."

All the pain and heartache of the past two years boiled up in Sally. The sorrow and loneliness welled over, and in her mind she was shouting at the man she loved so much.

"What's the point? Life sometimes gets so empty without you!"

Her father's smile did not change. "That's all the more reason for you not to give up, Sally. Get angry at me if that's what it takes to make you fight. You can do it, love, I know you can. Think of what it would do to your mother if she lost you, too."

"Oh, Dad, I loved you so much!"

"And I loved you, Sally, never forget that. And remember, you can still fight."

"It's hopeless!"

"Hold on, Sally, hold on."

His face wavered and started to recede into the distance, the voice in her mind growing fainter.

"Don't leave me, Dad. Don't leave me!"

"I'll never leave you, Sally, never. Even if you can't see me, I'll still be with you." His face faded to nothingness, and his voice was the merest echo of a whisper. "I'll always love you, Sally, always ..."

A rough hand bit into Sally's shoulder and shook her violently awake.

"Bad dreams, eh?"

Dazed, she looked up into Tony's glittering green eyes. "Well you won't be having many more, good or bad." He stood over her in the small boat, his legs astride as he rode easily with its motion in the deep strong swell of the waves. "You made me look a fool, and I don't like that. So I thought I'd wake you up to say goodbye, and to tell you what to expect." His thin lips twisted cruelly. "This boat's sinking slowly, so you'll suffer in the sun before you go down." He moved to the bow of the boat and started to pull the rope in, hand over hand, drawing it close to the launch so that he could put his hands on the stern and heave himself up on deck.

Once there, he turned to sneer down at Sally lying in the bottom of the small craft in a jumble of seawater, canvas and ropes. He held the mooring rope in his hands.

"You'll probably get your name in the newspapers — girl drowned in mysterious accident at sea — but you won't be around to read them." He undid the rope and threw it into the boat. "Another mystery of the sea, eh? The sea keeps her secrets, girl, she tells no tales."

With a last mocking wave to her, he turned and went forward.

She heard the powerful motors start up with a roar and watched dumbly as the long sleek shape of the launch started to move away over the ocean, slowly at first, then gathering speed.

85

Sally didn't watch it go for long. She was on her hands and knees in the bottom of the boat, groping about in six inches of water for the drain hole through which the water must be coming. A surge of water against the palms of her hands located it for her, and she quickly stripped of her sweater and wadded it into a ball then rammed it home, blocking the inlet at least partially. With her feet she pressed it down more securely, satisfied at last that it was as tight as she could make it.

She splashed seawater over her face, shocking herself into awareness. Her arms were heavy and her legs were weak, but her mind was alert and determined. She would not give up! No matter what, she would not lie back and accept her fate.

Faintly she seemed to hear a whisper, "Good girl."

The sun was beating down pitilessly, reflected off the brazen sea in a dazzling hot yellow glare like the inside of a furnace.

Sally knew she must cool herself down and find some protection from the fierce rays that were burning the will out of her.

Amongst the sodden jumble of old canvas in the bottom of the boat, she found one piece that she could separate from the rest. Stiff and heavy with the seawater it had absorbed, she had to struggle to pull it over her head and shoulders, but she managed it. The coldness of it shocked her, but the dimness beneath it was welcome after the glare outside. Even the stinging of salt against her hot dry skin helped to combat the listlessness which lurked so eagerly around her, waiting to take her over.

Shading her eyes with her hand, she poked her head out from her makeshift shelter and scanned the horizon in all directions. There was nothing but water, a sullen slow swell which moved the little boat lazily on a sea that looked like molten brass.

There was no breath of wind, and no trace of cloud in the harsh unblemished sky.

Sally had to keep busy, do something, anything, to keep herself from going to sleep. Feverishly she fished among the spars and ropes swilling around in the bottom of the boat and found another short length of canvas which she folded into a makeshift basin.

It took every fibre of her willpower to do it, but Sally scooped the canvas along the bottom of the boat capturing a cupful of the sea-water then tipping it over the side.

Painfully slowly she repeated her movement, deliberately and mechanically. A cupful at a time, she set out to bail the boat dry.

How long she kept it up, she never could remember, but she did force herself to repeat the movement over and over again, long after her brain told her she didn't have the strength to continue.

Her lips were cracked and dry and the temptation to plunge her face into the sea and gulp down the cold water was almost irresistable. Instead, she licked her salty lips almost continuously, trying not to think of ice cold drinks and the water she could almost taste in her throat.

Sally tried to picture her school friends in her mind, tried to recall every line of poetry she had ever learned and finally went over and over in her thoughts the words of every song she had ever sung.

From time to time she roused herself from her torpor to gaze around her, praying that there would be something on the horizon, anything that could help her.

When she first saw it, she didn't realise what it was, that low, grey mass on the horizon. Then, as her eyes passed the message to her brain, she had one brief flicker of hope, soon dashed as she realised that what she was seeing was mist.

How cruel could fate be, to give her hope like that, then snatch it away again so quickly?

She watched the mist steal softly across the water towards her, stealthily, like a beast of prey stalking its quarry.

A few wispy tendrils reached out greedily towards her and she felt the damp coolness on her face and bare arms. Then the main body of the mist enshrouded her, blocking out the sun and covering her face, her arms and her hair in a million tiny droplets of cold, clammy moisture.

Cautiously at first, she licked her lips tasting the sweet coolness of fresh water. She left off her bailing to lick her arms, her cracked tongue scooping the moisture into her mouth and easing her parched throat.

It wasn't much, but it gave Sally new heart.

"That better, is it, lass?" The deep, gruff voice so close made Sally's heart leap madly. "Saved many a poor seaman, that has."

Wildly she looked round her in the mist, but there was no one there.

"Now we'll have to see what we have here."

Sally was alone, but that voice, so loud and confident, sounded as though it were next to her.

"We're friends, Sally." A woman's soft voice whispered. "We've come to help you."

Sally put both hands to her forehead. She'd read about people going mad from too much sun and she'd read about people going mad from drinking salt water. Was that what was happening to her? Was she going mad?

She stood up, rocking the boat violently, looking round her for help, but there was none.

"Sit down, girl!" The gruff voice had the ring of command. "We can't help you if you go overboard."

"I won't listen! I won't!" She pressed her hands over her ears to shut out the sound of madness. "I'm imagining it, that's all!"

"Please sit down, Sally, please." The woman's sweet voice coaxed. "We can only help you if you help yourself."

Sally sat on the spar across the boat which served as a seat for an oarsman.

Something was happening to the mist! The sinister grey was taking on a golden hue, as though the sun were trying to penetrate it to get to Sally. It swirled and writhed around her as though it were being stirred, whorls of gold and tendrils of orange spinning faster and faster around her making her eyes ache and her head spin.

She closed her eyes, pressing the palms of her hands over them to block out the mad kaleidoscope of colour, but she couldn't block out the voices.

"Sally?" The sound was soothing to her tortured mind. "Open your eyes, Sally and look at me." There was warmth and gentleness there, an aching tenderness, love and understanding all in a few quiet words.

Sally took her hands away from her eyes and stared towards the stern of the boat. Through the golden haze, she could discern a shape, a feminine shape, seated in the seat.

"Come here," the woman said, opening her arms so that Sally felt drawn towards her.

"Careful, lass." A tall, black-bearded man materialised out of the mist and held up a warning hand. "You don't want to go overboard, do you?"

A peculiar floating sensation stole over Sally, and she had the oddest impression that she had left her body behind as she carefully stepped down the middle of the small boat.

She looked down into the woman's face, oval shaped and soft with large blue eyes and a full mouth curved in a smile.

Sally was in a dream, a soft kind dream after the nightmare of the past few hours.

"Sit here, my dear." The woman motioned to the wooden seat beside her. "We do not have much time and there is much to do."

Sally could not take her eyes off the woman's face as she sat beside her. There was something so familiar about the face framed by long blonde hair. She was sure she knew that face, had seen it many times before. It was a face she could trust.

"Who are you?" Sally whispered.

"Please, my dear girl, do not ask questions." It seemed that the woman reached out and touched Sally's hand, but the girl felt nothing. "We must make good use of the time we have."

"Aye, lass." The tall, black-bearded man in the strange clothing of another time bent over Sally and fixed her with his gleaming black eyes. "We're going to make a seaman of you."

"I – I don't understand."

"Frighten you, do I?" His white teeth showed startlingly against his black beard when he laughed. "Maybe you'd take more kindly to someone nearer your own

90

age?" He stood upright and cupped his hands to his mouth. "Billy!" he shouted. "Billy Briggs!"

"Aye, cap'n." Now there was the small figure of a boy with spiky red hair and a freckled face standing next to the tall man and gazing up at him with mischief on his urchin's face.

"Got a job for you, Billy boy."

"Cap'n?" He would be about ten years old, small, thin and dressed in cast offs that were much too large for his small frame.

"Think you can rig a mast on this scow and get some kind of sail up?"

The urchin looked down at the mess on the bottom of the boat, his face which should have been smiling, creased by a frown. "I think so, cap'n."

"Good lad, Billy. Show the lass how to do it."

"The lass?" Billy's face was covered in dismay. "I don't like girls, cap'n." He scowled towards Sally. "You said you'd make me a proper seaman one day. Looking after females isn't a seaman's task."

"Billy," the captain scowled in turn. "A real seaman does what his captain tells him." He put his hand on the boy's shoulder and his tone was more gentle. "And rigging this old scow is a task for a real seaman."

"Really, cap'n?" The boy's face lit up. "If I do it will I be a real seaman?"

"Aye, lad, that you will."

The boy beckoned to Sally. "Here," he said. "You'll have to come amidships."

Sally turned her eyes back to the woman who smiled at her reassuringly. "We can only help you to help yourself, my dear."

Doubtfully, Sally started to get to her feet and found herself sitting on the spar at the front of the boat.

91

Now her body felt heavy, her arms leaden and her legs weak. She was thirsty again and her head ached intolerably.

Billy beckoned her.

"No," Sally said wearily. "I don't think I can stand."

"You must, lass, you must!" The captain's voice was urgent.

"Huh," Billy scoffed, his face scornful. "She won't even try."

It was annoyance more than anything else which straightened Sally's legs and got her on her feet, lurching and staggering as the boat swayed alarmingly under her.

"There." Billy pointed a finger at a small wooden box fixed to the flat bottom of the boat. "Take the cover off."

As Sally bent over to put her hands on the lid of the box, she nearly toppled forward but, from somewhere, she found the strength to lift the cover off and disclose a slot set into the timbers.

"The mast slots in there." Billy was smug as he aired his knowledge to a mere female. "If you get your legs on either side of it and lift it so ..." He stood astride the heavy wooden pole that lay in the bottom and bent over to grasp it with both hands. As he straightened up, his clasped hands came through the wood and Sally gave a little gasp.

"I won't be able to lift that." She stared down at it in dismay. "It looks so heavy."

Billy put both hands on his hips and stared at her, having to look up into her face. "Aren't you even going to try?" He snorted with disgust. "How am I ever going to get to be a real seaman if you won't even help yourself?"

92

"Please, Sally, please. You must try." At the sound of the woman's voice, Sally felt resolve flow through her. This might only be a dream, but even in dreams she wasn't going to give up.

She put one foot either side of the mast and clasped her hands around it, taking a deep breath before she strained and heaved at it.

"Good girl." Billy jumped up and down on his bare feet and clapped his dirty hands together as the heavy pole shifted then lifted, slowly tilting up as Sally strained and pulled, throwing her weight back to counterbalance it as it swayed for a moment before sliding gently into the slot in the timbers.

Sally collapsed on the wet boards gasping and sobbing for breath as the boat bobbed and danced, seeming to take on a new buoyancy now the mast was in place.

"No time to rest now, girl." The captain's voice was gentle as he urged her to her feet. "Plenty of time to rest when the scow's rigged."

"Rigged?" Sally shook her head. "But how?"

"You've got the hardest part over." Billy dropped down beside her, cross legged on the bottom of the boat. When he smiled, Sally noticed that his two front teeth were missing. "Now take those two pieces of rope and that spar there."

It seemed as though Sally's hands had a life of their own as they unravelled the rope and threaded it through pulleys, straightened out the sodden canvas and tied it to the spars she had sorted out from the jumble of odds and ends.

She secured the mainsail to the boom and attached the jib to the pulley, reefed the halyards to the gaff under Billy's expert guidance, never stopping to question how she knew what he was talking about.

93

At last it was done, the sails hoisted, slack and loose in the still air, Sally with Billy by her side, staring up at them in open mouthed astonishment.

"Did I do that?" Sally shook her head knowing this must be a dream."

"All shipshape, cap'n." Billy saluted the black-bearded man who smiled at him and patted his unruly hair.

The captain surveyed the rigging, limp in the golden mist, then turned his piercing gaze on Sally. "Whither now, ma'am?" His eyes twinkled. "Shall it be the Indies or mayhap a voyage round the Cape?"

"Chertsea," Sally gasped. "Back to Chertsea." It was a dream after all. Deep aching disappointment nagged at her.

"Now for the test of a real seaman." The captain did not notice her disappointment as he rubbed his hands together and looked down at the ragged urchin. "Think you're up to it, Billy?"

Bitter tears stung Sally's cheeks as she leaned forward and put her hand where she knew there was no mast, only a figment of her imagination. But her hand closed on wood!

She put both hands on the mast and tugged then pushed. It was solid, Sally's exertions rocking the boat from side to side.

She turned her disbelieving eyes on the woman who smiled at her warmly.

"It's really there." Sally knocked the mast with her knuckles, delighted by the dull sound of wood. "It really is there!"

"Course it is." Scornfully Billy swaggered up to her. "But you couldn't have rigged it without my help."

"It's real enough, girl." The captain's voice was gentle.

94

"Now it's up to young master Billy to make it worth having."

"You mean it, cap'n? You're really going to let me try?" It was though the lad had been given the greatest prize imaginable. His face lit up with sheer joy as he fumbled inside his ragged shirt.

"What do you think, m'dear?" The captain turned to the woman in the stern.

"I think Billy Briggs is a real seaman at last," she laughed, and Billy did a little jig, scarcely able to contain his pleasure.

"Sit in the stern, lass." The black beard split to show the white teeth. "And hang on to the tiller tightly."

Sally's heart lifted and she laughed out loud. "I've got a chance, a real chance," she breathed. "Oh, how can I ever thank you?"

As she carefully inched her way towards the seat in the stern, the woman wavered and seemed to fade. "Fare thee well, Sally," she smiled, and there was sadness in that smile. "You'll know well enough how to thank us when the time comes."

"No!" Sally staggered as she reached out her hands to the woman. "You can't leave me now."

"We must, Sally, we must." Her strangely familiar face danced before Sally, the eyes shining with unshed tears. "But don't be sad, dearest girl, don't be sad." She was gone and Sally felt an ache of emptiness, a deep hurting sense of loss.

She dropped into the stern of the boat, her eyes clouded with tears. She felt she had lost something very precious, something irreplaceable.

A sweet, pure note sounded ringingly on the still air and Sally looked through her tears to see Billy, his chest puffed out with pride, his cheeks puffed out with air as he blew on a small, silver pipe he held to his lips. His image wavered as the note changed, soared clean and sharp and keen, thrilling Sally's ears and making the hair on the back of her neck stand up.

Tentative as the touch of a butterfly's wing, a breath of air stroked Sally's cheek and the mist, now fading to grey, wreathed and eddied. The sail, above her head billowed, flapped, then billowed again and the small boat hesitated then started to glide, slowly at first, through the water.

Billy still stood amidships, his legs spread, the single pure note sounding from his pipe as the breeze strengthened and the mist started to disperse.

"Billy Briggs!" The captain's voice thundered from nowhere.

Billy took the pipe from his lips. "Aye, cap'n." Then he looked over his shoulder and peered all round him as though looking to see whether he was being watched. He turned his head and looked at Sally.

"Thank you, Billy," she smiled.

Billy looked over his shoulder once more, then back to Sally. He grinned cheekily, then stuck his tongue out at her and vanished.

Chapter 9

Cruel Sea

The breeze was fresh and strong, filling the sail and sending the small boat skipping and bouncing over the waves towards the setting sun in the west – and towards land.

Sitting in the stern, with one arm wrapped around the tiller Sally tried to make sense of all that had happened in the last few hours.

Her head now cleared by the stiff breeze, Sally had almost convinced herself that she had been dreaming, although no dream had ever left her with such a poignant sense of loss, such a desolate feeling that she had said goodbye for ever to friends.

And surely no dream could explain the fact that she had rigged the sails. She stared at the heavy mast. It was unbelievable that Sally had lifted that on her own.

And there was the woman's face, those expressive blue eyes and that long blonde hair. It was a face Sally knew, a face she had seen many times, a face that was strangely familiar.

The wind gusted and the boat veered off course. Sally

97

leaned on the tiller and brought the bow back to point directly at the last dying rays of the sinking sun as it disappeared behind a dark mass rising out of the sea. How did she know how to do that? It was almost like having someone sit behind her telling her what to do.

The darkness was gathering now, and Sally began to worry once more. Everyone knew the sun sank in the west, so steering had been easy up until now. But Sally knew nothing about stars, and what if the wind shifted in the dark and took her off course?

Ahead of her, a light winked on and off, a bright eye staring out of the darkness. Then there was another light, so that there were two of them staring at her. They turned away, briefly showing as two beams and Sally knew what they were. They were car headlights. That dark mass was land.

She willed the small boat to travel faster over the water.

A sound ahead of her filled her with exultation, confirmation that she was nearly safe, the threshing of water breaking against a beach. It got louder, crashing and smashing, and soon she could see the white of breaking surf in the gloom ahead of her, the waves whipping themselves to foam against a rocky headland now cruelly visible as the moon came out from behind the clouds swiftly scudding across the sky.

Sally's excitement gave way to apprehension as she realised this was no simple beach. These were sharp, cruel rocks and the surf pounding against them, urged on by the same fresh wind as was filling Sally's sails, could easily pound the small craft to a million pieces – and Sally with it.

She threw her weight against the tiller, trying to turn

the dinghy but, in the grip of the incoming tide, the boat only slewed dangerously to one side, dipping as the wind drove the sail over, tilting the small boat so steeply that water lapped greedily over the gunwale.

Sally released the tiller and let the wind carry her forward almost into the white surf, bitter tears of anger stinging down her face at the thought of having come so far and done so much only to be beaten by the rocks and the tide.

No! She would not give up!

Hopeless though it might look, she was going to try and swim for it. Sally stood up in the boat, waited till the stern was up, and plunged over the back, reasoning that if she dived away from the vessel, there was less chance of it hitting her head.

The bitterly cold water knocked the breath from her body and she gasped involuntarily, swallowing a mouthful of the salt water, choking and smelling the sea in her nostrils. She could feel the undertow greedily tugging her legs deeper, trying to hold her, to keep her down there forever.

She kicked and she struggled using hands and feet to fight towards the surface, gulping in a great lungful of air when her face broke the water then feeling herself sucked under once more.

A dozen times she fought her way through to the air above before being dragged down again, her chest aching, her arms and legs stinging from the sharp rocks, scratched from their rasping contact with rough stone and razor sharp limpets.

Strength almost gone, she kicked down hard with her feet and nearly screamed aloud when something sharp drove into the soft flesh of her foot.

She had touched bottom.

Buffeted by the angry waves, she stood erect, her shoulders breaking surface, her face in the sharp clean air. Pounded to and fro, scarce able to stand, she drove one foot after the other up and out of the raging maelstrom of foaming, swirling surf, boiling and seething with insane rage at the loss of its prey.

For a brief instant she forgot her exhaustion in the sheer exhilaration of being free of the weight of water. Ignoring the pain of the rocks and shells under her feet, she ran out of the tide on to the blessed, unbelievable solidity of the land.

Her legs gave way beneath her and she fell full length on the sharp shingle, heaving in great greedy gasps of air, feeding her aching lungs with the oxygen they so badly needed.

For minutes she lay there, scarcely able to believe she had survived, shivering and trembling in the cold air.

Then, making one final demand of her spent body, she forced herself to her feet and – thinking only of one step at a time – stumbled unsteadily up through the coarse grass that bordered the beach on to the tarmac of the road that ran above it.

Lights dazzled her and she was hardly aware of the squeal of rubber on tarmac as a car screeched to a halt only inches from her.

There was a hand on her shoulder, concerned eyes looking into her face, an arm round her waist then – unbelievably – warmth and the feel of a rough towel drying her face and hair.

Something scalding hot was pressed into her hands, and there were other hands round hers as it was guided to her lips. She choked and gagged as the hot bitter liquid burned over tongue and into her throat, spilling out of her mouth and over her chin.

"Not too much at once." Hands pulled the mug away from her lips. "That's right, you breathe deeply."

Sally did so, and with each deep draught of air, her trembling subsided, the disjointed noises and lights formed a pattern, gradually taking on meaning.

She was in the back of a car, a blanket round her shoulders, gentle hands rubbing her hair with a towel. Hot air was blasting out of a vent on the floor and the vague white shape in front of her eyes became a beaker with a yellow sun smiling at her from its side.

"Are you feeling better now?" Sally turned her face and looked into the eyes of a middle aged woman staring anxiously at her. Sally managed a smile but, as yet, no words.

"You'd better drink some more of that coffee." The woman's hands closed round Sally's and gently raised the beaker towards her lips. Gratefully, Sally sipped the hot, bitter beverage, feeling its warmth spread a glow through her whole body.

"What happened? Did your boat sink?" The woman put both hands on Sally's shoulders and stared deep into her eyes as though trying to read the answers there. "Was there anyone else aboard?"

"No." Sally squeezed her eyes shut tightly. The coffee and the woman's questions were dispersing the fog that surrounded her. "I – I was in the boat by myself." She pressed the hot beaker against her cheek, her returning memory bringing with it a sense of urgency.

"Chertsea!" The woman was startled by the intensity in Sally's voice. "I must get to Chertsea at once."

"I think it would be best if I took you to the cottage hospital for a check up first."

101

"No! You've got to take me to Chertsea – please. It's very important that we get there right away."

"Well," the woman glanced at her watch. "It would take a good half hour to get to the cottage hospital and we can be in Chertsea in ten minutes."

"I'll explain as we go, but we must hurry, please!"

The woman studied Sally's face carefully, then came to her decision. "There's some dry clothes in that suitcase. They may not fit very well, but you change into them." She slid out of the back seat, closing the door behind her, then got behind the driving wheel. "You can tell me all about it on the way to Chertsea."

As they sped through the night to Chertsea, Sally told her story to the woman, whose name was Mrs Trent. She knew she had convinced her when Mrs Trent started to fire questions at her, and it was no bad thing, for it helped her make the story rational so that it could all be understood first time.

When they pulled into Chertsea Old School and parked behind the police car in the yard, Sally knew exactly what she was going to say.

"Sergeant Harris, thank goodness." Sally sighed with relief as the tall policeman opened the door to her.

"Sally!" He drew her inside. "We've all been worried sick about you. We even brought your mother up from London."

"Mum?" Sally stared up at him wonderingly.

"We'd better tell her you're all right." He took her by the shoulder and steered her firmly towards Mrs Hay's office.

"I'll see Mum in a minute, sergeant, but first I've got to tell you about the smugglers!"

"Smugglers?" the smile faded from his face. "What smugglers?"

"They've got a fast launch and they're bringing some stuff ashore here, at Chertsea, tonight."

"How do you know all this?" His sharp eyes studied Sally's face as she started to spill out her story.

"We were warned to stay away from the coast road by this old man at Little Chertsea station, but then we came that way, anyway and ..."

"Wait just a moment, Sally." Mrs Trent who had come in with Sally put her hand on the girl's shoulder. "You're tired and excited, love, and you're not making a lot of sense. Let me tell the sergeant." She turned to face the policeman. "Sally told me the whole story on the way here, and if you want to check whether she's speaking the truth or not, get on to your headquarters and ask them if there's been a report of a girl drifting in a small boat out at sea."

Sergeant Harris's face was grim as he pulled out his radio. "Yes, we did get that report through. That's why we were calling off the search for Sally here in Chertsea.

"That was a diversion to keep you away from here tonight."

"Sally, you go in and see your mother. Let her know you're all right." He walked quickly towards the door, opening out the aerial on his radio as he went. "I'll want to talk to you in a couple of minutes so don't go to sleep or anything."

He went through the door, talking into his radio and Sally went in to the office.

There were tears and there were kisses from Sally's mother and even Miss Parson dabbed at her eyes genteely with the corner of a lace handkerchief.

Then Sergeant Harris was back, no longer the jovial bobby, but now crisp and efficient.

"I'm sorry about this, Mrs Barnes," he said to Sally's mother. "But we've got an emergency here. I've got to get down to the coast road right away – and there's a lot of questions I have for Sally. Would it be all right to take her with me in the car? I know it's a bit much after all she's been through, but she could be a great deal of help to us. Naturally, I'd like you to come as well, just to keep an eye on her." He turned to Sally. "Do you think you can manage to stay awake for another hour?"

"Try and keep me away," Sally smiled.

Chapter 10

Midnight Meeting

They sat in the police car, with the lights and the engine turned off, on top of the cliffs looking down over Chertsea harbour as Sally, in the back seat with her mother, told her story to Sergeant Harris.

As she had with Mrs Trent, Sally did not mention how she had managed to rig the mast and sails on the small boat. With it pounded to pieces on the rocks down the coast, nobody was going to know she had had the sails rigged anyway.

"What I don't understand is how you got back to shore, Sally." Her mother held Sally's hand tightly.

"Just luck, I think." Sally tried to shrug the matter off. "The main thing is that I made it."

"Thank goodness." Her mother squeezed her hand.

"You should be very proud of your daughter, Mrs Barnes," the sergeant said. "I'd be proud of her if she was mine."

"Don't you have children of your own, Sergeant Harris?" asked Sally.

"Not married, Sally," he said, sounding almost as if he regretted the fact.

He glanced at his luminous watch. "The other cars should be here in a few minutes now. I hope they get here in time."

"What time is it?" asked Sally's mother.

"It's nearly midnight," the sergeant answered. "I'm hoping the villains try to make their drop after midnight. After all, there's not a lot I could do on my own if they try before the others get here."

"What about the trawler?" Sally asked

"The navy should be taking care of that. It's that fast launch you told me about that worries me. I don't think we've got anything in this area that can catch it if it gets out to sea."

"It's supposed to be going back to the trawler after that Ahmed has been ashore . . ." began Sally.

"Ssh!" Sergeant Harris silenced Sally with his upraised hand. "I can hear something."

They listened intently, hardly breathing.

Faintly at first, more a sensation than a noise, Sally heard a distant throbbing far out to sea. Then the throb of other engines drowned it out as two darkened cars nosed their way quietly along the coast road towards them.

Sergeant Harris slipped out of the car and disappeared into the darkness with the uniformed officers from the other cars. The night was still, save for the throbbing of the launch's engines as it came close inshore.

Then even that sound ceased, and the quiet was broken only by the swish of water breaking on the shingle below.

Five minutes ticked agonisingly past while the heat drained from the car and Sally began to appreciate the thick woollen sweater and the quilted track suit trousers she was wearing.

The blast of a whistle shattered the stillness of the night, and bright dazzling beams of light pierced the darkness, flickering hungrily to and fro over the beach below and locking on the launch lying about twenty metres off shore.

Momentarily the men on the deck of the launch were frozen, like actors in the spotlight, then they burst into violent action. One of the men hacked at the rope securing the anchor chain with an axe, severing it in two blows while the other disappeared into the bridge. As the powerful engines roared into life, another beam locked on to the dinghy halfway between the launch and the shore, the men in it rowing furiously to get back to the power boat.

But they were too late.

Slowly at first the launch moved forward, the water at its stern lashed into a creamy froth. Then the bow came up as it gathered speed, cutting a wide arc through the dark water as it circled, accelerating all the while then straightening up to head out to sea, the front rising further as the throbbing engines pushed it faster and faster, cleaving through the surf.

There was a shrill scream of fear and Sally's eyes flickered back to the dinghy lurching from side to side in the wake which the launch had thrown up. One man threw out his arms and toppled into the sea before the dinghy turned turtle. Another man and the cargo of crates were thrown into the choppy dark water.

Still gaining speed, the launch headed out to sea, the bow now well up, great white waves forming under the speeding hull.

Something was wrong. In the clutch of the lights, the launch seemed to falter and hesitate, the bow pointing even higher out of the water. Then the whole craft was free of the sea, lazily tilting to one side as it cleared the waves. It turned further and further over, the bow dipping down, biting at the waves, catching as the stern rose and describing a crazy spinning cartwheel, splintering and grinding into a million pieces with a sickening wrenching scream of tortured wood and metal.

An orange mushroom blossomed briefly with a muffled thump, then vanished beneath the sea. There was a glimmer of gold in the depths of the water for less than the space of a heartbeat, then darkness.

Restlessly the beams of the police searchlights probed at the darkness, picking out the struggling forms of men threshing and splashing amidst the debris on the oil stained water.

Now Sally was aware of other sounds, the shouting of men, the sound of whistles and another sound, like the beating of the wings of a giant insect.

A flashing light overhead indicated the presence of a helicopter which hovered above the police cars for a few seconds while the pilot spoke to the police on the radio then, nose down, headed out to sea, a huge vengeful dragonfly.

Voices came closer.

"You can't prove I had anything to do with it, Harris. I was out for a walk, that's all. It's a free country, isn't it? I know my rights. In this country, you've got to prove me guilty, and that's something you can't do." The voice was one Sally remembered with fear and loathing.

"Come on, Tony, save us all a lot of time and trouble. You make it difficult for us and we'll throw the book at you." Sergeant Harris's deep voice sounded almost friendly.

"I was out for a walk, that's all. I was nowhere near all that disturbance when your Gestapo jumped on me." Sally's skin crawled as the hateful voice came closer.

"What about the girl, Tony? She was just a kid."

"Girl? What girl? I don't know nothing about no girl. You trying to fit me up for something?"

Sergeant Harris brought Tony close to the car, his arm locked around the other man's arm, and forced his face close to the window. "That girl, Tony. The one in the back of the car."

Tony glanced in the back of the car and the blood drained from his face. His eyes bulged and his lips went grey and tight. Opening and closing his mouth soundlessly, he strained away from the window, his eyelids twitching.

Sally leaned closer to the window, her eyes burning accusingly into his green eyes.

Tony found his voice in a terrified scream. "Keep her away from me! Keep her away!"

"I don't think we can do that, Tony." Sergeant Harris looked regretful. "Unless you tell us what we want to know."

Tony thrust his knuckles into his mouth and gnawed at them in an effort to stem the scream, his eyes flickering from side to side, his grey face beaded with sweat. He mumbled something.

"I didn't quite catch that, Tony. Did you say you wanted to ride in the back with the girl?"

"No!" Tony shouted. "Keep her away from me!"

Sergeant Harris frowned. "Maybe you'd rather go back out to the trawler, to the reception Ahmed and Dietrich had planned for you? It would certainly save the taxpayer a lot of money if I let you lot settle with one another."

109

"What?" Tony was speaking to the sergeant, but his fascinated gaze never left Sally's face. Then his eyes became crafty, and a look of relief passed over his twitching face. "That's not her," he said. "That's her sister – or someone who looks like her." He was triumphant now. "You tried to trick me, copper." The sneer was back on his face as he tore his eyes away from Sally. "And don't try that old trick about Ahmed and Dietrich trying to double cross me ..." He stopped and a flash of cunning crossed his features. "And I don't know any Ahmed or Dietrich."

Sally put her face close to the glass of the window and stared accusingly at Tony whose flickering eyes came back to rest on her face.

"The sea does sometimes give up its secrets," she mouthed through the window.

"I – I ..."

"Doesn't matter now, Tony. You've given yourself away by recognising the girl. You might as well come clean."

"But how ... how did she ..."

"Want her to tell you?"

"No! Keep her away from me. I – I'll tell you, I'll tell you everything – if you'll keep her away from me."

"That's nice." Sergeant Harris winked at Sally before hustling Tony away.

He was back within minutes, on his own. He had a huge smile on his face. "Superstitious lot, these fishermen," he laughed. "Now," he turned to Sally and her mother in the back seat. "Shall we go back up to the school? With any luck, they'll have the kettle on."

Chapter 11

The Captain's Curse

It was nearly noon when Sally woke to bright sunshine and an empty room.

She stretched luxuriously in her bed, wincing as her scratched and bruised legs rubbed against the sheets, but feeling absolutely relaxed and rested.

Getting out of bed, she padded across to the window, to look out on the bright warm day.

Two figures caught her eye as they strolled, walking very close together, over the lawns that surrounded the old school. Her heart leapt as she recognised her mother and with her – just for an instant it had looked like her father – was the tall sergeant dressed in civilian clothes. They looked well together, and Sally knew her father would have approved.

A quick shower and she would be ready for whatever that day had to bring.

It was while she was combing her hair that she glanced in the mirror and, with a quick, poignant stab of anguish, recognised the face that was looking back at her as being like that of the woman in the boat. No wonder the woman had been so tantalisingly familiar, she was Sally's double. So the whole thing had been a fantasy after all? Panic stricken, Sally's subconscious must have summoned up an image of the one person in the whole world who could help her at that moment – herself.

The disappointment was keen, as though Sally had had something precious taken from her. Her blue eyes were moist as she finished combing her blonde hair. It was as well that she hadn't told anyone about what she thought had happened in the dinghy.

Dressed, she went downstairs to be greeted by her mother, for once lost for words as she tried to tell Sally how terrified she'd been. The tears did start once more, but Sergeant Harris produced a large snowy white handkerchief and handed it to Mrs Barnes. "We can't have that, Susan," he said gently – very gently. "We don't want any red eyes when the newspaper people get here."

Then he put his arm around Sally and smiled down at her. "I expect you want to know how last night ended up?"

"Oh, yes."

"You were almost asleep when we got back here last night, so I don't suppose you'll remember the state of play when you went to bed?"

"I remember the launch overturning, and I remember you bringing that horrible Tony to the car. After that, it's all a vague jumble, getting back here with that nice woman who gave me a lift, Mum being here, Mrs Hay and Miss Parson . . ."

"Right. Number one, we got them all. Every last one of them. The Royal Navy captured the trawler and released the three men from the village who were being

112

held as hostage. Your friend Tony couldn't stop talking and told us everything we wanted to know. Funny that, no matter how tough they are, all fishermen are super-stitious. Every so often he kept going on about the sea having her secrets."

"The leader, Ahmed – did you get him?"

"Found him in the sea begging us to rescue him. Real hero he was. Took two shorthand typists to keep up with him, he told us so much. Named all his contacts, where they picked the stuff up, how much they paid for it. We arrested the two men at Little Chertsea station. They were using the old buildings as a warehouse."

"What about the launch? What happened there? I thought they were going to get away."

"Funny that." The sergeant frowned. "Some naval frogmen went down this morning to see what had hap-pened. It was most peculiar!"

"What did happen?"

"There's an old wreck been lying on the bottom there for over two hundred years. In all that time it's never moved, but last night, part of it floated to the surface – and wrecked that launch." He laughed. "So it was thanks to the *Sally Hanson* those men were captured. It's almost as though the ship was getting revenge on the smugglers for using the legend of its ghosts to frighten people off."

"That is peculiar." Sally's mother put her arm around her daughter. "Do you know, I believe that your great grandmother was called Sally Hanson? I wonder if there's any connection?"

Sally thought of the woman's face and *knew* there was a connection.

"Do you feel up to seeing those reporters now?"

Sally nodded her head without speaking. So that was

113

why the woman on the boat had had tears in her eyes. Sally must be some far distant descendant.

She squared her shoulders and got ready to meet the people from the newspapers. They could ask all the questions they wanted, but this was something she was going to keep to herself, her own special secret.

Sally had asked the woman how she could ever repay her, and the woman had told her that she would know how when the time came.

Sally had the strangest feeling that the time was coming.

The reporters kept her busy till tea time and as they asked their questions and took their photographs, Sally slowly came to realise just how large the operation had been to smuggle goods into the country. She had assumed it was a small, local gang of smugglers earning a few pounds by by-passing the internal revenue, and bringing small consignments of alcohol or maybe tobacco into the country. But as the reporters talked, she gradually came to realise the enormity of the operation. It was a huge international crime ring dealing in firearms or anything that would make money.

No wonder Sergeant Harris was so pleased with himself.

Eventually, the crowd left and Sally had her first chance to be alone with Joanna and Katie. Both girls were eager to know every detail of Sally's adventures, but she only told them as much as she had told the police and the press. There were some things you didn't share, not even with your best friends.

They got permission to stroll down to Chertsea, as long as they didn't keep Joanna out too long.

It was like an entirely different village.

There were the same pastel painted cottages, but now they gleamed in the sunshine, their doors open welcomingly. Even the front gardens seemed to be full of colour, and scent.

As they passed one beautiful garden at the foot of the hill, an old man hobbled down the garden path towards them.

"Hey, you," he called.

Sally sighed. Katie cast her eyes up to the heavens and Joanna pretended not to hear.

"You, miss, you with the long blonde hair."

"Pretend you didn't hear him," Katie whispered out of the corner of her mouth. "I don't think I can take any more strange happenings."

"I've got something for you, Sally. It is Sally, isn't it?"

Reluctantly, Sally turned towards him.

"Here." He handed her a bunch of roses, red white and lemon. "I was one of the men on the ship." His wrinkled face shone with glee and his mischievous old grey eyes twinkled under his shaggy grey brows. "Though, if I'd known you was as pretty a girl, I wouldn't have needed an excuse to give you flowers."

Sally buried her face in the blossoms and breathed deeply. "They're beautiful."

"Aye, lass, but beside you three, they're not all that special." Chuckling, he hobbled back up his garden path, and the three girls continued on down the hill.

At the quay, there were three women standing in a group, chatting and laughing – a complete contrast to the silent, secretive folk Sally had seen in the village before.

When the friends passed, the women looked round, smiling at them. Sally recognised the woman from the

115

general store, but the worry was gone from her face, and her eyes sparkled with good humour.

"I wanted to thank you," Sally said. "For trying to warn me."

"Nay, lass, it's us folks as should be thanking you." The woman took Sally's hand in both of hers and squeezed it warmly. "My father was one of the three they took, so I'll always be in your debt."

"Could you give me some information?"

"Anything you want to know."

"Is there any sort of grave, or monument, to the people drowned on the *Sally Hanson*?"

"Aye, in the churchyard – though it's not a pleasant place, our churchyard."

"Oh?"

"Some say it's since those twenty three poor souls were buried there all those years ago." She linked her arm through Sally's and started to walk along the front. "But I think it's the soil."

"What is?"

"The blight. Nothing grows in the churchyard, not properly, that is. In fact, it's so bad that nobody's been buried there for over a hundred years."

Joanna looked interested. "You mean there's a curse on the place?"

"Some say the captain of the ship was still alive when they brought him ashore ..."

"According to what I read they were all drowned."

"Mayhap your book's right. You know how old wives' tales abound in fishing villages."

"Tell me the story." Sally was intrigued.

"Well, they say that Chertsea was a very prosperous village in the old days. If you look around, you'll see that it was once much bigger than it is now."

116

"What happened?" breathed Katie. She would be getting a notebook out and taking notes soon.

"After the wreck of the *Sally Hanson*, the village started to decline. There's those as say wreckers were at work that night, and they lured the ship on to the rocks. Anyway, the fishing fleet was lost at sea, lots of families left, and the village shrank and shrank. If there was an epidemic going anywhere it would find its way to Chertsea. Then there were floods and fires. All manner of ill fortune."

"You say there was a curse on the village. How did that come about?" Joanna's eyes were big and round.

"They say the captain of the ship was washed ashore still alive. A fine big man he was, by all accounts. Accused the villagers of wrecking his ship. Went mad, they say, when his wife's body was brought to him in the church. Laid a curse on all the villagers and the village."

"Then what?" For someone who didn't like ghost stories, Katie was very inquisitive.

"Then he died. Just sat down and died. I suppose he had nothing left to live for."

"Poor man." In her mind's eye, Sally could see a tall, black-bearded man with white teeth and flashing dark eyes.

"Wasn't there something about a child and a flower?" Joanna asked.

"Oh, that." The woman laughed. "You know how those storied grow through the years ..."

"Tell us," Katie urged.

By now they had reached the wrought iron gates that led into the churchyard, and the woman paused. "I'll tell you out here. I may be only a superstitious old woman, but I don't like going in there." She pointed at the gates.

117

"I don't like the looks of it either." Katie shivered.

"When the captain's wife was brought to the church, one of the village children had placed a bunch of flowers on her breast. He saw the flowers and, in the great voice of his, thanked the child. He is supposed to have said – though, mind you, I think this was put in later so people wouldn't all leave the village – that on the day another mark of kindness was made to him or his wife without thought of gain, then that day the curse would be lifted."

"And what about the ghosts? Have you ever seen them?" Joanna asked.

"Ghosts, girl?" The woman laughed. "You don't believe in ghosts, do you?"

"But what about the stories?" Joanna was disappointed. "There's lots of stories about people seeing the ghosts walking through the village."

"Woman and girl I've lived here for sixty years, and never heard of anyone seeing ghosts."

"What about the curse on the churchyard?"

"As I said, I think it's something to do with the soil. There's lots of places where things don't grow well – and they haven't all been cursed by dying sea captains." She turned to walk away from them. "On your way back, call in at my cottage for some lemonade and some cake. It's the pink cottage at the foot of the hill."

"Where's the grave?" Sally called after the woman.

"You can't miss it," the woman called back. "It's straight in front of you as you go through the gate – by the big dead yew tree. There's some as say the yew tree died the day they were buried there, but I think it just died of old age."

As the woman disappeared down the lane, Katie shivered and looked in her direction longingly.

"Sally," she said, very quietly. "I don't think I want to go in there. I never did like cemeteries."

"What about you, Joanna?" Sally stopped as she saw that strange look on Joanna's face again.

"I think this is something you ought to do alone, Sally." Her eyes were faraway and dreamy. "Katie and I will go back now and leave you."

"Oh, you're only thinking of the cake and lemonade that woman promised us." Katie linked her arm in Joanna's. "But I'm glad I don't have to walk back down this lane by myself."

Sally wasn't listening to them. She was staring into the churchyard in fascination.

She hardly noticed as the other two girls left her and went back down the lane leaving her alone in front of the wrought iron gates.

Chapter 12

Roses for Remembrance

The churchyard was a depressing place. Neglected and gloomy, the old tombstones were leaning at crazy angles with weeds growing between them, sour and yellow, as though the sun had never penetrated there. Even the ancient stones were covered in algae, their inscriptions unreadable under the poisonous-looking green coating.

The few trees were stark and bare, as they would have been in midwinter and the sparse grass that grew in places was tall and strangely unhealthy.

Straight ahead of Sally, one huge black yew dominated the far end of the churchyard, its blighted branches entwined around one another as though in agony.

One plain grey granite stone beside the yew was not covered in algae. It stood aloof, clean and cold and alien in that place of dark and decay.

Although the lettering had been chipped into the stone over two centuries before, Sally could still read it as well as though it had been done only last week, even the archaic spelling giving her no trouble.

Above the long list of names was a stark, plain statement

of fact: "Here lie the mortal remains of the twenty three souls who perished in the wreck of the merchant ship, *Sally Hanson*, cast aground on Chertsea Point on the night of July 7th, 1736, Anno Domini."

Then followed a list of names beginning, "Richard Hanson, master. Sally Hanson, the wife of the above. Charles Frogmore, first mate ..."

Sally read down the list of names, and tears sprang to her eyes as she saw on the bottom. "A child of ten, cabin boy, whose name is unknown."

Poor Billy Briggs. Not even his name on a stone to keep his memory alive.

Suddenly she realised she still held the roses in her hands. Tears spilling down her cheeks, she laid them on the ground at the foot of the stone, kneeling down on the sparse grass to arrange them, inhaling their rich fragrance so foreign in that dark, cold place.

Her heart beating faster, she stared at the blossoms, then counted them. There were twenty two fully opened flowers and one tight red bud. With trembling fingers, she picked the bud from the other blooms and held it up to the stone.

"This one is specially for you, Billy," she whispered.

The silence of the churchyard was shattered by the raucous cackle of a magpie, a loud irreverent chattering that sounded as though it was jeering at her.

From somewhere behind the stone, it flew into view perching on top of the grey granite and looking down on Sally with bright, inquisitive eyes. Its tail bobbed up and down jauntily as it swaggered up and down on top of the stone, scolding and clucking at the girl below who looked up with wide blue eyes.

"They're going to give me a reward for helping to

121

catch those smugglers." Sally was talking to the magpie and — somehow — it didn't seem ridiculous. "And the first thing I'm going to do is get something added to the inscription on this stone."

The black and white bird stopped its chattering and seemed to be listening to Sally.

"I'm going to have them add, 'William Briggs Esquire, Seaman'."

Behind Sally a blackbird called and somewhere in the churchyard, another one answered.

Enraged, the magpie strutted up and down on top of the stone, chattering madly, his feathers now illuminated by a stray beam of sunshine which had found its way into the graveyard, turning his sober black and white plumage into a rich blue and green display of finery.

Sally jumped as a squirrel skittered over the graves a few feet from her.

And suddenly the churchyard did not seem such a depressing place after all. Sunshine was all around her and the air was filled with the sound of birds. A white butterfly with bright orange tips to its wings danced past her on the light summer breeze.

The magpie hopped down from the top of the stone into the yew tree and started tugging at the branches with his strong beak. He was pecking at a fresh green shoot growing there.

As she turned to look round, a flash of light caught the corner of her eye. Something bright and shining was reflecting back the light of the sun.

She walked over to it and stooped to pick it out of the ground, a silver whistle, bright and shining. She had seen one before, once in a museum and once on a small boat out at sea – it was a bosun's pipe.

"It's something you brought in here, isn't it?" She waved the pipe at the magpie who had now lost interest in her as he preened his sleek plumage.

Smiling, Sally almost skipped back down the path towards the wrought iron gates which guarded the entrance to the churchyard.

Her heart was light, and the world was a wonderful place, for Sally knew that no matter what the future brought, no matter how hopeless things might seem at times, she would never, ever feel alone again.

Now she had to make sure her mother felt the same way. Who knows, there was a certain police sergeant who might just fit the bill as far as that was concerned!

Behind her in the churchyard, the magpie was strutting importantly up and down in front of the grey granite stone, almost as though he was trying to picture what the new inscription would look like.

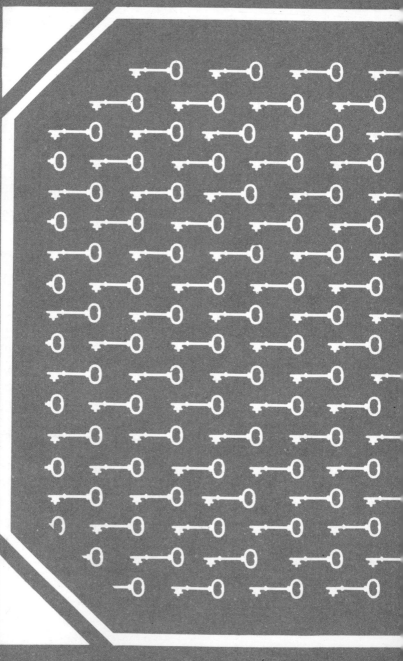